W9-CCA-122

LITERATURE AND LANGUAGE DEPARTMENT
THE CHICAGO PUBLIC LIBRARY
400 SOUTH STATE STREET
CHICAGO, ILLINOIS 60605

THE END OF THE ROAD

MAXIE AND STRETCH MYSTERIES
BY SUE HENRY

The Serpents Trail

The Tooth of Time

The Refuge

THE END OF THE ROAD

A Maxie and Stretch Mystery

SUE HENRY

AN OBSIDIAN MYSTERY

Obsidian
Published by New American Library, a division of
Penguin Group (USA) Inc., 375 Hudson Street,
New York, New York 10014, USA
Penguin Group (Canada), 90 Eglinton Avenue East, Suite 700, Toronto,
Ontario M4P 2Y3, Canada (a division of Pearson Penguin Canada Inc.)
Penguin Books Ltd., 80 Strand, London WC2R 0RL, England
Penguin Ireland, 25 St. Stephen's Green, Dublin 2,
Ireland (a division of Penguin Books Ltd.)
Penguin Group (Australia), 250 Camberwell Road, Camberwell, Victoria 3124,
Australia (a division of Pearson Australia Group Pty. Ltd.)
Penguin Books India Pvt. Ltd., 11 Community Centre, Panchsheel Park,
New Delhi - 110 017, India
Penguin Group (NZ), 67 Apollo Drive, Rosedale, North Shore 0632,
New Zealand (a division of Pearson New Zealand Ltd.)
Penguin Books (South Africa) (Pty.) Ltd., 24 Sturdee Avenue,
Rosebank, Johannesburg 2196, South Africa

Penguin Books Ltd., Registered Offices:
80 Strand, London WC2R 0RL, England

First published by Obsidian, an imprint of New American Library,
a division of Penguin Group (USA) Inc.

First Printing, November 2009
10 9 8 7 6 5 4 3 2 1

Copyright © Sue Henry, Inc., 2009
Map copyright © Eric Henry, Art Forge Unlimited, 2009
All rights reserved

OBSIDIAN and logo are trademarks of Penguin Group (USA) Inc.

Library of Congress Cataloging-in-Publication Data
Henry, Sue, 1940–
The end of the road: a Maxie and Stretch mystery/Sue Henry.
p.   cm.
ISBN 978-0-451-22604-4
1. Women dog owners—Fiction.   2. Dachshunds—Fiction.   3. Suicide victims—Fiction.
4. Alaska—Fiction.   I. Title.
PS3558.E534E63 2009
813'.54—dc22   2009021237

Set in Adobe Garamond
Designed by Alissa Amell

Printed in the United States of America

Without limiting the rights under copyright reserved above, no part of this publication may be reproduced, stored in or introduced into a retrieval system, or transmitted, in any form, or by any means (electronic, mechanical, photocopying, recording, or otherwise), without the prior written permission of both the copyright owner and the above publisher of this book.

PUBLISHER'S NOTE
This is a work of fiction. Names, characters, places, and incidents either are the product of the author's imagination or are used fictitiously, and any resemblance to actual persons, living or dead, business establishments, events, or locales is entirely coincidental.
    The publisher does not have any control over and does not assume any responsibility for author or third-party Web sites or their content.

The scanning, uploading, and distribution of this book via the Internet or via any other means without the permission of the publisher is illegal and punishable by law. Please purchase only authorized electronic editions, and do not participate in or encourage electronic piracy of copyrighted materials. Your support of the author's rights is appreciated.

R04228033876

With the author's sincere thanks,

this one is for

the many generous and helpful people

at the end of the road in Homer,

from the top of the kill to Land's End,

who patiently answered many questions

and provided information that greatly

assisted in the creation of this book.

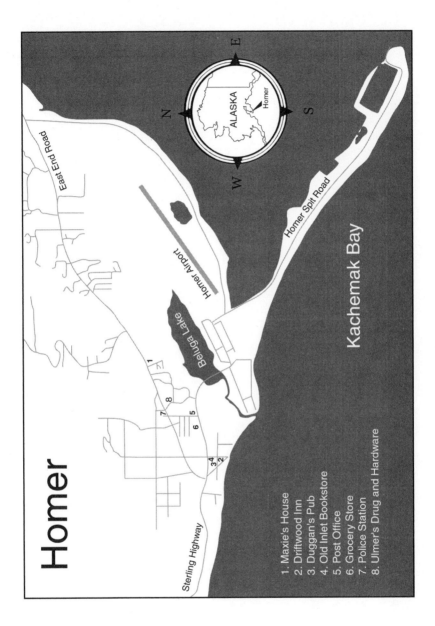

Homer

Sterling Highway

East End Road

Homer Airport

Beluga Lake

Homer Spit Road

Kachemak Bay

N

E

S

W

ALASKA

Homer

1. Maxie's House
2. Driftwood Inn
3. Duggan's Pub
4. Old Inlet Bookstore
5. Post Office
6. Grocery Store
7. Police Station
8. Ulmer's Drug and Hardware

ONE

I WOKE LATE ON FRIDAY, THE FIRST OF NOVEMBER, having stayed up late with a favorite book that I was reading between trips to the door in answer to the intermittent summons of several pirates, a robot costumed in cardboard boxes, a couple of skeletons, and a steady stream of other trick-or-treaters whose attire defied analysis in combination with their winter boots, coats, hats, and gloves. "Trick or treat!" they called out when I opened the door and gave them back a "Happy Halloween!" along with their expected treats, a couple of which fell into the depths of large, optimistically offered pillowcases.

One of the earliest visitors was a small blond fairy wearing blue wings over her down jacket and clinging shyly to the hand of her father—my next-door-but-one neighbor, Jack Gifford.

"What do you say to Mrs. McNabb?" he prompted her, after I had dropped several candies into the plastic pumpkin she carried in her other hand.

"Thank you," she told me in just over a whisper.

"You're very welcome, Shelly," I told her, then watched with a smile as they went down the drive, remembering how my own two children had loved dressing up for Halloween.

The tradition was clearly alive and well in Homer, Alaska, and I enjoyed the parade of costumed spirits that mittened expectantly on my door. For the first time in several years, I had not driven my motor home down the long Alaska Highway in the fall of the year to spend the winter in warmer southern climes. During the school year, RV parks are often short on children and long on retired senior citizens. So it made me feel very much at home to recognize the children of my neighborhood, now grown a little taller than I remembered them.

Rolling over that morning after All Hallows' Eve, as my Daniel liked to call it, I sat up and swung my feet over the side of the bed to feel for the slippers I had left on the floor beside it. Instead, one foot brushed the warm back of my mini dachshund, Stretch, already wide-awake and waiting attentively, holding down one of my blue fuzzy slippers with both paws as if he expected it to attempt an escape.

"Good morning, lovie," I told him, giving him a pat before reaching to retrieve the slipper and standing up to put on the fleece robe I had hung on the bedpost before retiring. "I know it's late and you want to go out, don't you? Well, let's go down and you can do your business while I start the coffee."

I scooped him up and carried him down the stairs and into the hallway next to the kitchen.

Unlocking and opening the door just enough to let him scamper out into the cold first of November morning, I was reminded by the icy breath of the early Alaskan winter that it was arriving as anticipated, though we had yet to see snow. So I quickly closed the door after him and stepped to the nearby thermostat to turn up the heat, which I normally lower several degrees at night, preferring to sleep cool, but not cold.

With the coffee gurgling cheerfully through a filter into the pot, I turned to fill Stretch's water and food bowls, then went back to the door in response to his scratching on the other side. Cold weather meant he didn't take time to tour and inspect the yard before wanting to come back inside—his usual practice before the temperature drops significantly.

Though the weatherman had predicted the possibility of clouds rolling in later in the afternoon, it was bright and sunny outside that morning and the thermometer outside the kitchen window read thirty-four degrees—just above freezing.

Sitting at the table with a mug of coffee and an English muffin liberally spread with peanut butter and peach jam made earlier in the year by a friend, I enjoyed the view to the south over the wide waters of Kachemak Bay that were sparkling in the sunshine and the Kenai Mountains rising beyond, white with a line of snow halfway down.

It was, I decided, a perfect morning for a walk.

"Want to go walkabout?" I asked Stretch, who had finished his breakfast and gone to lie down by the sliding door to the back deck, where he could keep an eye out for any squirrel or bird trespassing in the yard.

Though walkabout was one of my deceased husband Daniel's Aussie terms, which I had adopted, Stretch, originally his dog, knew immediately what I meant and was on his feet in agreement with the idea.

"Good. We'll stop by the post office and pick up the mail, then go out on the spit and walk the beach for a bit. Okay?"

His enthusiastically wagging tail was answer enough, so after a quick shower, I pinned my hair up in its usual twist, noticing a bit more gray at the temples, dressed warmly, and put his red plaid coat on Stretch. Though it was sunny I knew we could count on it being cool, especially with the breeze that usually whispers in across the waters of the inlet and flows over the long, narrow arm of land that forms the spit. This narrow natural extension of land reaches five miles out into the bay and holds the marina and port of Homer, along with condominiums, small tourist shops now mostly closed for the season, huge parking lots, and the Land's End hotel and restaurant.

After pouring the rest of the pot of coffee into a thermos, I added sugar and a splash of milk, and took it with me, along with a bottle of water and a plastic bowl for Stretch.

We were on our way shortly in my small car, Stretch riding shotgun in the basket that hangs from the back rest of the passenger seat, a considerable and welcome boost for a small dog who likes to be able to see out the window.

I drove west on East End Road through Homer's main downtown intersection where it becomes Pioneer Avenue, then turned left on Heath Street and went down the hill to the post office, parked and went in, leaving Stretch in the car. There was little mail, a couple of fliers of no interest to me, which I discarded into a recycling bin left for that purpose, and took only the latest issue of *Alaska* magazine and two envelopes, one large, one small, back to the car with me, glancing at the return addresses as I walked.

The large one was my bank statement, which I tucked away in

my day pack without opening. There would be plenty of time later for that.

The smaller one bore a familiar address, and I tore it open as soon as I was back in the car with the engine running to keep us warm. Inside I found a bright Halloween greeting card from Jamie, the daughter of a now-departed dear friend in Colorado, with whom I had kept in touch after meeting her the year before. Along with the card was a photo of her small son dressed in the cowboy costume he had evidently worn trick-or-treating, and she had written a few lines to let me know that she had recently moved from Salt Lake City into the house her mother had left her in Grand Junction and I should address any mail to her there. This pleased me, for Sarah's historic Victorian house was a real treasure and I knew Jamie would be happy living in it with her boy. She included an invitation to stop and stay with them any time I was traveling through Colorado.

"We'll have to drop her a note and let her know we're staying home this winter, won't we?" I asked Stretch, who gave me a glance before returning his attention to the people who were passing on their way in and out of the post office.

"Okay," I told him. "Forget the *we*. *I'll* write the note. Let's go find a place to walk, yes?"

I backed out of the parking place, turned the car and drove us out of the lot and onto the highway that would lead to the spit in a mile or two.

Alaskans have long said that if the small community of Homer is not "the end of the road" in our state, at least "you can see it from here." It is perfectly true that once you arrive in Homer, there is nowhere else to drive but back up the Kenai Peninsula on the highway you came down on; through Soldotna and Cooper Landing, over Turnagain Pass, and down to Girdwood, where Alyeska Resort provides some of the best skiing available in the country, then on another fifty-plus miles to Anchorage, a total of just over two hundred and twenty miles.

They also say, with Russia on the other side of the Bering Sea, that it is "as far as you can go without a passport."

I love living in Homer and was not unhappy to be spending the winter in my hometown. I've been there all my life and watched it grow from a village to a fair-sized town. Still, it maintains its casual, small community attitude and reputation as a fishing and art center, drawing hoards of visitors in the summer months—tourists that crowd the hotels, campgrounds, restaurants, shops and art galleries, museum, and Sea Life Center, and fishermen who charter boats to go out in search of the giant halibut that secrete themselves in the deep waters of the bay and larger inlet.

The Homer Jackpot Halibut Derby was started in 1986 by the Chamber of Commerce and from Memorial Day to Labor Day each year draws participants from all over—many from the Lower Forty-eight. In the summer of 2007 the largest halibut caught weighed 358.4 pounds, was too large for five men to pull into the boat, and won the fisherman who caught and brought it in to be weighed a prize of $37,243. But it was not the largest on record—a monster caught in 1996 had tipped the scales at 376 pounds.

During the winter months Homer turns into a much quieter place and the locals take a deep breath and have time to visit with their neighbors and friends. Many small shops, especially those out on the spit, close until the next tourist season and their owners settle down to enjoying life in one of the warmest spots in the state north of the southeast panhandle. Besides being at the end of the road,

Homer is sometimes called "the banana belt," with winter temperatures ten degrees or more higher than Anchorage, which is northeast
of us at the head of Cook Inlet. But then, according to a bumper
sticker I noticed recently, it is also called "a quaint drinking village
with a fishing problem."

———————

About a block from the post office the highway angled south to
cross the slough, curved east and became Ocean Drive, then, shortly,
south again as Homer Spit Road, and passed the airport before dip-
ping onto the spit itself. I drove us out approximately three-quarters
of its length, with ocean water on each side, until it widened and we
reached the large lot that overlooked the marina to the east. Except
for a few cars and trucks at the south end it was almost empty, a
condition totally different from that during some summer week-
ends, when in a crowd of vehicles I might have been lucky to find a
space to park anywhere but far at the north end.

I pulled in and parked closer to the road than to the marina,
walked around to take Stretch out of his basket, lower him to the
ground, and attach his leash. After locking the car, I pocketed the keys
and shouldered my day pack, and we headed across the highway toward a path that would take us down to the west beach, a dozen or so
feet lower than the road.

As we started down it the horn of a vehicle honked behind me
and I turned to recognize a friend who was a nurse at the Homer
South Peninsula Hospital and was evidently on her way back into
town from somewhere farther out on the spit. She pulled over to the
side of the road, let the motor idle, rolled down her window, and
offered a smile as I walked up to say hello.

"Maxie! What are you doing in Alaska? I thought you'd be long gone to somewhere down south for the winter."

"Hi, Becky. I decided to stay here this year," I told her. "Guess I was homesick for the place."

"You're a glutton for punishment," she warned. "There'll be snow soon, and below-zero temps. Better think again."

"Already put the motor home into storage in Anchorage for the season. Guess I'm stuck."

"Well, in that case, can you come tonight for spaghetti and an evening of dominoes and Farkel?" she invited. "Linda's here—flew down from Anchorage yesterday for a night or two, and it'd be more fun with three of us."

"Love to," I agreed. "What time? And I'll bring the wine, okay?"

"Great. Come on over—oh—whenever. Five. Six. Whatever works for you. I'll see you then. Now I gotta run to meet Linda for lunch. I left her at Ulmer's looking for a new filter for her fish tank and a glass top for the coffeepot. See you later."

She was gone with another wave, this one out the window, as Stretch and I turned again to go down to the beach.

The tide had been on its way out since early that morning, leaving a wide shingle of wet sand in its wake. The sea was fairly calm, though the breeze was strong enough to blow a bit of spray off the surface of each low incoming wave.

A couple of glaucous-winged gulls were riding the air currents in wide, sweeping circles over the water. Like the eagles, they would stay all winter. I was surprised, however, to notice a solitary arctic tern, with its black cap and red bill and feet, huddled close on the sheltered east side of a battered log that had drifted in and been stranded when the tide went out. Usually these attractive birds migrate south in the fall to escape the cold and return in the spring. They have forked tails and long pointed wings trimmed in black on the posterior edges and I love to watch their graceful flight, swooping in over the beaches where they nest, sometimes in colonies, among the rocks and grasses of the beaches of Kachemak Bay.

Reaching the bottom of the sloping path on the dry part of the beach, I turned us south to walk along behind a row of little shops with steep pointed roofs that had been built on a platform over heavy pilings that raised them up to be level with and facing the road, their backs to the sea. When all the visitors and fishermen leave at the end of the tourist season the proprietors of these small businesses close them up tight and retreat to their homes in town for the winter. Only a few larger, more solidly built structures remain open—a restaurant or two, the Harbor Master, Coast Guard, and Alaska State Ferry Offices, and the Land's End Resort, for instance.

I let Stretch off his leash and he trotted immediately over to explore among the pilings that supported the now closed shops above us. Somewhere there he found a stick that he deemed acceptable and brought it back to drop at my feet, looking up at me expectantly. He's not much into the game of fetch, but once in a while he will play for a few minutes before something else attracts his attention and he leaves me holding the stick, so to speak. This time it lasted four or five retrievals before he gave it up, curiosity aroused by a gull that landed close to the water on the wet sand left by the retreating tide, but it took off again with a resentful squawk at his approach.

We walked for the better part of an hour. Or at least I did.

Stretch must have covered several times my distance in his explorations and investigations. Finally, when I began to feel cold, I sat myself down on another abandoned log, my back to the sea breeze, and pulled the thermos out of my day pack, along with his bowl and the bottle of water I had brought along. Noticing what I was doing, he came scampering back and waited politely while I splashed some water into the bowl, then lapped it up thirstily. I gave him more and poured myself a thermos cap of the breakfast coffee, which I sipped as I watched him drink his fill, then lie down to rest at my feet in the shelter of the log.

It had been a good walk, but it was turning truly chilly as the anticipated clouds rolled in from the west and the sun, already low in the southern sky that late in the year, disappeared behind them. The wind had grown stronger and now that the tide had turned the incoming waves were breaking farther and farther up the sandy shore, significantly more spray blowing from each crest.

Farther down the beach I saw an eagle perched atop an old piling with its back turned to the gusts that ruffled its feathers. It was one of many that come to the end of the spit, where a woman who lives in a small one-room house has fed them for so many years that, though I'm sure she has a name, everyone just calls her the Eagle Lady.

All but one of the gulls that had been riding the wind high overhead had vanished into shelter.

"Well, intrepid explorer of beaches, are you ready to go home? It's getting downright cold out here."

Stretch stood up in response to the word *home*, waiting for me to get myself together and start.

After drinking the last swallow of the coffee I had poured, I shook out the last drop or two and replaced the cap on the thermos, tucked it back into the day pack with Stretch's water bottle and bowl, got to my feet and headed for the hill that would take us up again.

There were more grasses beside that more southern path that we took up to the road and they were rustling storm warnings to each other as they bent eastward, away from the cold air that tossed them down to brush semicircular patterns in the sand.

Stretch had picked up another stick somewhere late in his last investigations. He sneezed and dropped it as he breathed in some of the wind-borne sand that flew over the ground at his level. Leaving it where it lay, he trotted up the hill in record time and stood at the top looking down, as if to say *Come on, we don't have all day, you know.*

At times I think he actually believes he is responsible for me and that I simply could not possibly make it without him to supervise.

TWO

When I reached the top of the path next to the road I snapped Stretch's leash to his collar and we began to walk together along in front of the seaside shops, all closed and secured for the winter. As we passed, I read a few of the more than a dozen signs: The Spirit of Alaska Native Crafts, North Country Halibut Charters, White Wave Gifts, Across Alaska Adventures, Halibut King Adventures, Rainbow Tours, and Central Charters.

Facing these on the other side of the road were more small shops at ground level: The Better Sweater, Brown Bear Photo Safari, Homer Spit Gifts, and Forget-Me-Not Gifts—the last with a sign in its window that read, "Closed for the season. See you in the spring. Stop by our town location just uphill of the post office."

North of these was a much larger two-story building, stained a warm golden brown that accentuated its bright green metal roof. It housed the Coal Point Trading Company with its Fresh Seafood Market and gift shop, which I noticed was open and offering espresso as well. Now decidedly chilled, I considered that for a moment or two, but gave it up. There was coffee to be made at home, where we could warm up inside.

In front of the building was a tall pole with arrows attached top to bottom that pointed in all directions and gave the mileage to such mixed locations and distances as Cape Horn 9503, Anchorage 235, Seward 180, Beck's Saltry 6, Bering Sea 700, Ferry Office .04, Addie's 50ft, Halibut Cove 6, and Mt. Iliamna 58. As always, in passing, it made me smile at the sense of humor of the pole's creator.

As we came to the end of the row of shops on pilings, ready to cross the road, I was reaching into my coat pocket for the keys to the car when the leash went slack as Stretch suddenly stopped short in front of me. Off guard, I almost stumbled over him, but looking to discover what had caught his attention I saw a man sitting at one of the three or four picnic tables on the platform that supported the shopping area. He was facing the road, watching us pass, with a tall paper cup between his hands on the table in front of him— evidently some of the espresso offered across the street at the Trading Company.

His hair and forehead were hidden under a blue baseball cap with a bill, and he had zipped his heavy gray coat up under his chin. Under the table I could see a pair of brown work boots below his jeans-clad legs. A pair of heavy leather gloves and a wallet lay on the table in front of him.

That late in the year we have very few tourists, and this person's dress told me he was probably a working man, maybe a hand on one of the cargo ships that during rough weather sometimes come into the calmer, deep waters of the bay that are protected by the spit, or wait their turn to load whatever is waiting to be shipped. Most floating cargo comes into Alaska at Seward, where it can be loaded onto freight cars or trucks and transported on to Anchorage and Fairbanks. Points farther north that are off the road or rail systems are serviced by air. What we can't grow or produce in Alaska—and there are a lot of things that fall into that category—also comes in overland on the Alaska Highway, by plane from a wide variety of sources, or by sea all the way up the coast of British Columbia and the Alaska panhandle. Given his appearance, my first guess was that he had arrived on one of the latter and was perhaps waiting for that ship to be ready to start its long run back down to the Lower Forty-eight.

"Hello," I called, seeing that he was watching us. "A bit chilly to be sitting outside, isn't it?"

He nodded and smiled. "Yeah, but I wanted to take a look at the famous Homer Spit, so I hiked out from town. Didn't realize it was quite so far, so I'm warming up a little before starting back. It's very quiet out here."

"Always is this time of year," I told him. "The hoards of tourists desert us, shops close for the winter, and, as you can see by the emptiness of the harbor, many of the local fishing charter companies put their boats in storage. In the summer this place is busy as an anthill. Now it's pretty much just the permanent residents in Homer."

As I talked, Stretch was tugging on the leash, having decided he wanted to inspect the man at the table at closer range. After one particularly assertive tug, I gave in and allowed it, walking out onto the platform with him.

"This is Stretch, my insatiably curious dachshund," I told the seated man. "He's harmless—just wants to check you out and say hello."

"Well, hello there, buddy," the man said, reaching down to give Stretch a couple of pats and a rub at his ears, which he loves—and expects—and which almost guarantees his immediate approval and friendship.

As I watched them get acquainted, I considered this new and unknown person, who seemed pleasant enough, and finally extended a hand. "Now that you know my dog, I'm Maxie McNabb—Homer resident since I was born."

"John Walker," he responded with another smile, reaching with a hand warmer than mine from the hot coffee he had been holding. "Nice to meet you, Ms. McNabb."

"Just Maxie," I told him, feeling that his name rang a vague bell somewhere in my memory.

"Okay," he said and grinned. "Nice to meet you—Maxie."

"You hiked out here?" I asked him. "Didn't come in on one of the cargo ships, then?" I asked.

"Nope. I'm playing tourist. Caught a bus ride down from Anchorage Wednesday. Thought I'd like to see the Kenai Peninsula."

"The Homer Stage Line. Runs the year round and that's a pretty good way to do it."

"I enjoyed it. Lots of spectacular scenery before it got dark. I thought of going to Seward on the train, but I heard that Homer is supposed to be about as far west as you can drive in Alaska and wanted to see it. Seemed like the right place to me—the end of the road, right?"

"That's right, and we often say it's as far as you can go without a passport. One of our claims to fame—such as it is."

As we spoke I had noticed that the wind had risen to a whistle that was almost a howl around the shop buildings that partially shielded us from it. I could also hear larger waves crashing onto the beach out of sight below. It was quickly growing colder and the clouds that had rolled in were much darker. It seemed we might be in for some very stormy weather very shortly.

"Listen," I said to John Walker. "I'm heading back to town before this storm gets any worse. You really don't want to hike all the way back in the rain, do you? I'll be happy to give you a lift."

From under the bill of his cap he gave me a slightly twisted smile with a hint of humorous mischief in it.

"You sure you wouldn't mind?" he asked. "Sort of reminds me of Blanche DuBois—depending on the kindness of strangers."

I had to smile back at that as I assured him, "Absolutely sure. I'd be remiss in Homer hospitality leaving you to the mercy of what looks like a nasty blow coming in. Besides, now that we've introduced ourselves, we aren't total strangers, are we? Come on. That's my car just across the road."

He stood up and swung his legs over the bench that was part of the table at which he sat, and I realized that he was taller than I had anticipated and was looking down at me from perhaps three or four inches. Sitting at the table, the coat he wore had made him seem heavier than the slender build with broad shoulders that standing up revealed. I judged him to be somewhere in his forties, and from the look of his callused hands he had done heavy work of some kind, maybe construction, or something like it. He reminded me suddenly of my first husband, Joe, the fisherman I had buried at close to the same age. His hands had revealed his livelihood, too, scarred with the constant handling of ropes and lines, hooks and knives, that are necessary to the profession.

John picked up his gloves and stuffed the wallet into a hip pocket with one hand as he took up his cup with the other. He drained it quickly, tossed it into a nearby trash can, and followed me. As we hurried across the road the first fat drops of rain splattered down on our heads, making us glad to escape into the car as quickly as possible—Stretch and I in front, as usual, and John behind Stretch in the backseat.

As we traversed the narrower part of the spit back toward town the wind was strong enough for me to feel it shoving at the car, but not so much that it was an impediment to driving. Once in a while, when a bad storm blows in at high tide, they close the road to traffic, but that is rare. By the time we went up the hill to where the road turned left into its dogleg I had switched the windshield wipers on, but once we were off the spit into a more sheltered area the wind eased, hastening off to harass people elsewhere that were more exposed and, therefore, easier targets.

"Where are you staying, John?" I asked as we crossed the Slough Bridge, wondering whether to follow the Sterling Highway west or turn right at the first light and head up to the main street.

"At the Driftwood Inn," he told me. "In a room that's like a tidy cabin on a boat—very narrow, with not much floor space, but warm and comfortable enough. They're nice people and offer good coffee in the morning. I've spent most of my time outside anyway, exploring the town. But there's a good pub just across the road."

"Duggan's. I know it. Yellow building with shamrocks on the front."

"That's it."

I turned left to go a block down to the hotel.

"And there's the bookstore I found yesterday," he said enthusiastically as we passed it. "What a great discovery—crammed full of new and used books in every category you can think of."

"Andy's place—the Old Inlet Bookshop. I love it—get lost for hours sometimes."

"Right again. I found a couple of Patrick O'Brian's sea stories that I'd missed. This kind of weather discourages sightseeing, so I think I'll curl up on the bed in my room, or on the comfortable-looking sofa in the lobby by their fireplace, and read the rest of the day away. I'm relieved not to be out on the spit, many thanks to you."

"No thanks necessary. Reading's pretty much what I have in mind for myself this afternoon. You can eat at Duggan's."

It took only a few minutes to turn another corner and pull up in front of the Driftwood Inn, where John climbed out, came around, and leaned down to the car window with a smile.

"Thanks, Maxie, for the ride and the company. I really appreciate it."

"You're more than welcome," I told him. "If you have questions or need help, my number's the only McNabb in the phone book."

"That's nice of you. I'll remember it."

As I considered being truly hospitable and inviting John for supper, I suddenly remembered that Becky expected me for the evening, so instead I asked how long he intended to be in town.

"Haven't decided," he said. "The bus goes back to Anchorage on Monday and Wednesday mornings, so I'll be here through the weekend at least, maybe longer." He hesitated thoughtfully, then gave me an almost wistful half smile and said slowly, "Who knows? I like it here so far—interesting place—friendly people. Maybe I'll decide to spend what's left of my life at the end of the road."

"Some people have come for a visit and done just that," I told him, thinking his comment was an odd way of putting it. I would have said *the rest of my life*, not *what's left*.

He watched as I turned the car and gave me a wave as I pulled into the street, heading back the way I had come. As I turned the corner, I looked and saw him gone and realized that I had never asked John where he came from.

Before going home, I stopped at the grocery store and, after picking up half a case of wine in their attached liquor store, I spent half an hour wheeling a cart through the aisles for items I either needed or that caught my fancy.

Like the post office, the grocery in Homer is as much a community meeting place as anywhere in town and a visit to either can turn into a social occasion at times. In the produce aisle, I ran into Karen Parker Bailey, who, of course, wanted to vent frustration about the work required after moving back to Homer from Hawaii, with all the unpacking of boxes and arrangement of furniture involved.

"It's more than I can manage," she complained. "I can't do much with the pain I'm still suffering. Would you have time to help, Maxie—like you did in Hilo?"

Quickly I crossed my fingers behind my back before telling the lie that assured her I *did not* have the time, remembering the job of sorting, packing, and literally taking over to get her household goods ready to ship home, after the death of her husband, and a fall down a couple of steps that had broken both her left forearm and ankle. Knowing she wasn't anywhere near as disabled as she claimed, that it had been several months since her accident and, bone now healed, casts off, she was not exhibiting any real need for assistance, but rather her usual reluctance and aversion to any job that required much effort—along with an unquenchable craving for sympathy.

Wheeling the cart on past, I left her frowning resentfully after me as I ignored her second plea and moved along to select the vegetables I needed to create a pot of stew that I intended to simmer slowly through the next afternoon: onions, celery, carrots, and potatoes. In the meat department I picked up a package of stew beef and, in the frozen food section, some packages of corn, chopped broccoli, green beans, and a half gallon of peppermint ice cream. From there I rolled the cart to the bakery to add two fresh loaves of French bread and a chocolate cake to the collection.

Perhaps I would call the Driftwood Inn and invite John Walker for supper on Saturday—along with an acquaintance or two that he might enjoy meeting.

THREE

FRIDAY EVENING WITH BECKY AND LINDA was full of good food, conversation, and, of course, table games, which were really our excuse for getting together. The three of us have been friends for years and meet intermittently through the year, sometimes with another friend or two.

Since Becky and I both live in Homer, we are more often at her house or mine. At least once a year Linda arrives from Anchorage by car or plane, and we drive out to the spit to catch a water taxi, which ferries us across Kachemak Bay to Niqa Island.

There, high on a bluff, Becky has a cozy house that overlooks the most westerly of two shallow coves on Niqa Island. There we spend a weekend, or longer, taking walks, picking fat salmonberries for jam or jelly—if the season and weather are right—playing Farkel, Wizard, or dominoes in the evenings, sleeping long and eating well, laughing a lot, and simply enjoying each other's company.

In early November, however, the weather was too cold and

unpredictable for venturing across the bay, so we gathered at Becky's in-town house for the evening.

"Hey, Maxie. *Here you are!*" Becky said as she opened the door in response to my knock. "I tried to call twice. Once it was busy. Then I got no answer, so I knew you were on your way."

Linda came flying across the room to give me a hug.

"We were about to start without you," she teased, stepping back with a grin.

"Ahh, well—I knew you wouldn't start without me. I had a phone call from my son, Joe, in Seattle, that took a rather long time," I told them, setting the sack with two bottles of the wine I had promised on the kitchen counter and removing my coat to hang on a hook by the door.

"Problems?" Becky asked from the kitchen, where she was cutting cherry tomatoes in half and adding them to a salad.

"Nothing I can solve. You've both met his lady, Sharon, and know that she has her own travel agency in Seattle. At a conference a week or so ago she had an attractive offer of space in a downtown location to start a second office in Portland. The drawback is that she would have to move to Oregon for the next year or so to get it going."

"Portland's not too far away," Linda said. "About two hundred miles, I think. That's about the same as driving from here to Anchorage—a little less, actually."

Leaving one bottle of wine in the kitchen, I brought the other and Becky's corkscrew to the table, uncorked it and poured us each a glass.

"I know," I told her. "But with both of them working full-time—for Sharon that would probably mean six days a week to start with—how often are they really going to make that three- or four-hour trip? Joe's afraid it would break up their relationship."

"Oh, for Pete's sake!" Becky came from the kitchen to the table and set a bowl of spaghetti down on it with a thump. "Why doesn't he just marry the woman? She's a honey!"

"I like her a lot, too. I didn't suggest it, but maybe that's what he's sort of getting around to. It came up so suddenly that they're both adjusting to the idea of a big change. They've been living together for the last four years. He said she's pretty excited by the idea of expanding her business. I think he's afraid she might say no if it meant she would have to give that up. He's going to fly up tomorrow for the weekend, so I'll know more by the time he goes back."

"Well, keep us posted," Linda requested.

"I will," I promised as we sat down to eat.

———————

It was close to midnight when I got home. We had enjoyed apple pie for dessert, cleared the table to play three rounds of Farkel and two of chicken foot with the dominoes, and finished both bottles of wine. Altogether it had been a most satisfactory evening, as usual, with much laughter and conversation.

In the second half of my sixties, I am the oldest, with both Becky and Linda significantly younger, but the age difference has never mattered to any of us. Both of them are nurses—Becky at the Homer hospital and Linda at Alaska Regional in Anchorage. I always feel particularly safe with them around, just in case I should have a sudden heart attack or stroke, especially as Becky works nights in the emergency room and knows her stuff. Linda claims that when we're together I'm much more likely to die laughing than as a result of any serious medical condition.

————

Stretch knows the familiar sound of my car pulling into the driveway and was at the door to meet me with wags and wiggles, as if I had been gone a week and not just a few hours.

"You're a good and patient bitser, you are," I told him, dropping my coat over the back of a dining room chair, my purse on the seat of it, and leaning to give him the attention he was expecting. "You need to go out, I suppose."

He did. And, given the temperature, he made quick work of it.

I opened my eyes to the dark at just after seven the next morning. That time of year this far north the sun doesn't come up over the Kenai Mountains until around eight thirty, so there wasn't a hint of light outside. By Christmas it wouldn't rise until approximately nine o'clock and would set at three in the afternoon. Having been in the Southwest for the previous two winters, I found myself noticing and readjusting to the seasonal darkness I had accepted as normal all my life. It was an odd feeling—almost learning to be at home again.

After a quick wake-up shower, I ate a leisurely breakfast as I enjoyed watching the light grow over the mountains to the south through the sliding glass doors that lead onto the deck, which would soon be covered with snow. Then I washed up the few dishes before assembling the ingredients for the stew I intended to simmer slowly through the day.

Before putting it together, I called the Driftwood Inn and asked for John Walker, having made up my mind about asking him for supper that evening.

"Just a minute," the woman who answered told me. "He's right here having coffee. I'll put him on."

"Yes?" he said a few seconds later, sounding a bit hesitant and oddly cautious.

"Good morning, John. This is Maxie," I told him. "The woman you met on the spit yesterday."

"Oh, yes—my savior from the storm. Hello, Maxie."

"I'm having a few friends for supper tonight and wondered if you'd like to join us," I told him.

"I must assume you don't mean that literally," he said with a chuckle. "That they are to be served supper, not served up for it."

This bit of humor assured me that he would fit right in with the group I intended to invite.

"Well . . . ," I teased back. "Not being a cannibalistic sort, I hadn't considered the latter, but have beef for the stew I'm about to make."

"With that assurance, I'd be pleased to come, and thank you for the invitation."

"Good. My son, Joe, is flying in from Seattle about noon for the weekend. I'll send him to pick you up about five thirty, if that works for you."

"It does, but I can take a taxi if you'll give me the address."

"Not necessary. Joe'll be glad to come."

"I'll look forward to meeting him," John said. "And thanks again, Maxie."

———

Joyce Berman was also happy to accept my invitation and to hear that Joe was arriving from Seattle. She was originally from Helena, Montana, and had met her husband, Marty, when they both attended the University of Montana in Missoula. He had been a grade school and high school classmate of Joe's. They had been fast friends then and still were, so I knew Joe would be pleased to have them at my table.

I reached my friend Harriet Christianson at the library and was pleased to add her name to my list before making the last phone call, to retired fireman Lew Joiner.

Lew was a respected local character who had always been an avid fisherman and now spent the summers ferrying halibut hunters on his small charter boat. He was a cheerful soul and loved books about the sea almost as much as he loved fishing, so I thought he and John would probably get along fine.

My list of guests complete, I went to make the stew, after which I buttered and wrapped the French bread in foil so it was ready to warm in the oven later. With the stew simmering gently on the stove, I took Stretch for a quick walk up the road and back, then settled comfortably in my big chair near the fireplace to, as John had suggested the afternoon before, *read the rest of the morning away*—or, at least, until it was time to head for the airport to meet Joe's flight from Anchorage.

———

Leaving the edges brightly gilded, the sun was already slipping behind a bank of clouds on the western horizon when Grant Aviation's compact Cessna Caravan arrived on time at five minutes after one that afternoon. Son Joe got off with six other passengers and came striding into the airport waiting room with one small carry-on bag, already looking for me.

He crossed the room with an eager grin and gave an enthusiastic hug to his mother.

"Hey, Mom, I'm home," he said in my ear.

"So you are. And right on time, too," I told him as he released me.

"Trust Grant Aviation—they're seldom late," he said, glancing over his shoulder toward the ticket counter and lifting his free hand in a wave to the ticket agent, a girl he had known and dated in high school.

There are times that, with a turn of the head or a tone of voice, Joe reminds me so much of his late father that it makes me catch my breath and takes me back all those years to the time when I fell in love with and married Joe senior. What lovely and precious gifts our children give us when, all unknowing, just by being themselves, they remind us of times and people that have mattered most in our lives.

———————

By shortly after six the gathering was completed when Lew Joiner arrived last, handing me a bottle wrapped in a brown paper bag as he came in the door.

"Here's one for your wine cellar," he said. "And here," he continued, pulling two fat paperbacks from a pocket of the coat he had hung on one of the hooks by the door, "are a couple I hope you haven't read yet."

"I've not," I told him, examining the titles: *Rise to Rebellion* and *The Glorious Cause* by Jeff Shaara—both labeled as novels of the American Revolution. "But the author's name is familiar."

"His father, Michael Shaara, wrote a Civil War book I know you've read."

"Oh, yes. *The Killer Angels.*"

"That's the one. Jeff's written these two like fiction and you won't be able to put them down," Lew told me. "They're the whole war from the viewpoints of key figures like Washington, Adams, Franklin, Revere, Cornwallis, Lafayette—you get the idea."

"Sounds good. I'll read them right away. Just finished the book I was on and was in need of another. Thanks, Lew."

We had moved to the counter that separates my kitchen from the dining area, where I laid the books down and handed him a glass of Merlot.

"Yes, thank you, Maxie," he said. "Now, where's that son of yours?"

I was not surprised that Lew had brought me books, for we have shared a love of reading for years and often trade books back and forth, knowing each other's preferences well. It's an addiction we share with many others, for there are a lot of readers in Homer. When winter sets in seriously, probably close to half the town is reading on any given evening, if they aren't watching television.

I stood for a minute, looking around the large room that contains both living and dining areas—fireplace and comfortable seating at one end, table and chairs at the other. There is little I enjoy more than having friends and family gather for a meal at the house that was built by my first husband, Joe senior. Except for John Walker, everyone in this particular group had been guests of mine many times in the past and took pleasure in one another's company.

Lew had gone directly across the room to where Joe stood talking to John, and, introductions made, the three of them turned to examining the books that filled the shelves that rose on either side of the fireplace, in which a cheerful fire glowed.

Marty and Joyce were seated on the plump sofa that faced the fire, talking with Harriet, who occupied an easy chair at right angles to them. She had been a friend of Marty's mother, now deceased. Always a sort of adopted aunt to him, I knew she would be catching up on the welfare of his two small children and his job with the Sea Life Center in town.

Stretch, I noticed, was in his element, curled up on the middle cushion of the sofa, his chin on Joyce's lap to make it easy for her to give him pats and rub his favorite spots—ears and under the chin.

He switched to Marty when Joyce, noticing me looking in their direction, stood up and came across the room to join me.

"What can I do to help get food on the table, Maxie?" she asked. "If you're ready to ring the dinner bell, that is."

She was not kidding about the bell. Above the counter between the kitchen and dining area is a ship's bell that I hung up back in the day when I grew weary of calling my always scattered family to dinner. It still gets regular use, even to summon Stretch, who has learned it often means food and is no dummy when it comes to mealtimes.

"You can light the candles on the table while I retrieve the bread from the oven and put it in a basket," I told her. "Then you can ring it. Everyone can fill their own bowls with stew from the kettle on the stove."

In just a few minutes all were settled at the table, where, irrepressible, Lew glanced around with a twinkle in his eye.

"Good friends, good meat . . . ," he began, then hesitated, noticing the warning frown that Harriet, a dedicated churchgoer, was aiming at him, and concluded with, ". . . good . . . ah . . . *oh, good grief* . . . let's eat."

FOUR

MUCH LATER JOE AND I SAID GOOD-BYE to our company at the door as they left. It had been a good evening, full of spirited conversation and laughter, reminding me why I like living where I do and miss it often when I'm gone. I very much like traveling to new places in my motor home and the last couple of years had mostly been full of the pleasures of discovery, meeting new people and visiting old friends. But there had been a trade-off in leaving behind the place and people I know and love that left me a little lonely at times.

"Many thanks, Maxie," Lew said, turning to me as he zipped up his coat.

"You're more than welcome anytime," I told him. "And thank you for the books."

"Let me know what you think of them."

He had volunteered to give John a ride back to the Driftwood Inn, so they went out the door together after John added his gratitude as well.

"It was kind of you to include me," he said as I took the hand he offered. "You have a fine collection of friends and I enjoyed meeting them."

Harriet gave me a hug and hesitated long enough to remind me of a quilters' gathering at her house the following Thursday.

"Bring along that pattern book you found in Hawaii," she requested as she wrapped a woolly red scarf around her neck. "And that beautiful fabric you brought home as well, yes? The girls would like to see it."

Girls! Having met in grade school, most of us would always be girls to Harriet.

Smiling, I promised I would, and she was the last to go, closing the door firmly behind her after instructing us to stay inside where it was warm. "You'll freeze for sure if you wait on the step to wave us off this time of year."

Taking her advice, Joe and I settled at opposite ends of the sofa with the last of the wine half filling our glasses.

"Great evening, Mom," Joe said, kicking off his shoes and stretching his long legs out onto a stool to toast his toes in the warmth of the fire that was slowly becoming a heap of ashes and glowing coals. "It was good to see Marty and Joyce. Thanks for asking them."

"You're welcome, dear. I enjoyed them, too."

A thoughtful look took the place of his smile.

"Now," he said, "tell me about John Walker. He said you met and rescued him out on the spit yesterday."

"Not much to tell. I took Stretch for a walk and we met him as we came off the beach. He'd walked all the way out there and it was about to pour rain. He would have been soaked hiking back, so

I gave him a ride to town. Seemed the friendly thing to do for a visitor."

"Oh, I'm sure it was. He's a quiet sort—listens more than he talks—but I liked him. Doesn't say much about himself though, does he?"

"I guess not, but I didn't ask a lot of questions. I imagine that in a group of strangers—especially those that were here tonight and know all about each other—almost anyone new would mostly listen. When people get acquainted and comfortable they tend to loosen up, but some are more reticent than others."

"He was vague when I asked where he was from. Told me he was born in the South, but that his parents lived in several places when he was growing up. He doesn't have a hint of a Southern accent—or any accent at all that I could tell. Said he'd moved around a lot the last few years, doing mostly construction jobs. Mentioned New Orleans after the hurricane."

"Does it matter?" I asked, remembering my impression of John's callused hands.

"Not really—made me wonder, is all. Most folks are pretty forthcoming with information like that—unless they have some reason to hide it. Maybe he has one."

"Joe!" I said, shaking my head. "You're in forensics, and too used to looking for clues to the identity and behavior of *criminals.* Give John the benefit of the doubt. There are a lot of personal and perfectly legal reasons he might not want to be more specific—or interrogated, for that matter."

He stared at me for a long moment, eyes wide as he considered it.

"You're right, I guess," he finally agreed. "Sorry, Mom. I probably *am* allowing the job to creep into my thinking—and shouldn't."

"Good. Now, tell me all about you and Sharon—the Portland travel agency she's contemplating, and how you see it impacting your relationship. That's what you came up here for, isn't it?"

He gave me a long troubled look with a frown hovering in it before he answered, "Yes—I guess so. Partly I came just to get away and consider it. I thought it might be easier if I could get some perspective from a distance."

"What seems to be the source of the problem?"

"Well, obviously, it's going to split us up if Sharon decides to move to Portland. It's too far away to commute more than a couple of times a month, and that would mostly be up to me if Sharon's working six days a week at first."

"Be about like driving from here to Anchorage. That's not too far."

"Seems like it. I just can't make it work in my head."

"Does she really want to do this?"

"Yes, dammit! Or says she does."

His flash of anger so startled me that I sat silently staring at him for a long minute. He glared into the dying fire and wouldn't meet my eyes.

"You sound as if you think she's doing this on purpose just to rattle your world," I said slowly. "Is that what's bothering you? It doesn't sound much like Sharon to me."

He shrugged and shook his head ruefully, closely examining the level of the wine in the glass he was holding.

"No—I guess not," he admitted.

"But there's a piece of that mixed into your feelings somehow?"

"Maybe," he confessed. "I've been happy with things the way they are—or were. You know?"

"Stop for a minute and turn it around," I suggested. "If it was a job *you* wanted to take in Portland, how would that seem to you—and to Sharon? Would it be any different if you were the one who wanted to make a change?"

He frowned again, thinking about it. "I hadn't looked at it like that."

"I thought not. Might there be just a bit of chauvinism mixed into your thinking?"

"I guess it's possible."

We sat quietly for a few minutes, Joe clearly turning the idea over in his mind.

I thought back to Becky's reaction on hearing about the situation the evening before. *Oh, for Pete's sake!* she had said. *Why doesn't he just marry the woman? She's a honey!*

"Joe?" I asked him, finally, cautiously. "Don't take this as a suggestion from an interfering mother. You know that's not my style. But would it make a difference if you and Sharon were married? Part of a really good marriage is the freedom for both parties involved to be honestly themselves. It's recognition of the trust you share, that you know is basic and depend on. I think you're feeling threatened—that things are changing and out of your control. There! That's the word—*control.*

"And, by the way, you don't have to answer that question—just consider it, okay?"

He turned to give me a grin of approval.

"I will—am—have been," he told me. "But I appreciate the suggestion. Thanks, Mom."

"You're welcome. Now it's bedtime for me and the bonzer here." I stood and picked up Stretch, who had been dozing next to me, his chin on my knee. "Your room is ready for you."

"I'll be up in a few minutes," he told me and turned back toward the dying fire, a contemplative expression on his face.

"Good night, then, son. See you in the morning."

———

I didn't hear him come to his room upstairs, but went to sleep that night turning Joe's problem over in my mind. I had been lucky that both my marriages had been good ones, easygoing and well balanced in terms of decision making. Maybe it would have helped if his father had lived to be a sounding board for him. But, whatever resolution resulted from the current situation, I could only hope for the best for them both, and leave it to Joe and Sharon to solve, one way or another. He was not a child anymore and some things you have to work out and learn for yourself.

———

The smell of coffee drifting up the stairs—along with the scent and sizzle of bacon frying—brought me back to life the next morning. Stretch's bed on the floor next to mine was empty, so I knew he had joined Joe in pursuit of breakfast. Donning my robe and slippers, splashing some water on my face and running a comb through my hair, I went downstairs to find them both in the kitchen.

"Morning, Mom," Joe said with a grin. "I thought cooking bacon would probably bring you down."

"It did indeed, especially with someone else cooking. You've even set the table."

THE END OF THE ROAD

"That's because my mother taught me right. How do you want your eggs?"

"Over easy, as usual."

"You've got it. I've already let Stretch out and fed him."

I filled a mug with coffee and sat at the table, pleased to watch him moving around familiarly in my kitchen, thinking how nice it was to have him home, even briefly.

Saturday's storm was long gone, and glancing out the glass doors that led to my deck and yard I could see that the sky was blue and the waters of the bay sparkling in the morning sunshine. The mountains beyond looked sugar-frosted with snow halfway down— termination dust, as the miners called it in the gold rush days, as it signaled the end of the year's mining season. I knew it would soon make an appearance in Homer, but the day promised to be a pleasant one, if cool.

"What have you in mind for today?" I asked as Joe set a plate in front of me containing my eggs and bacon and an English muffin slathered with butter and Becky's peach jam.

Sitting down across the table with his own plate and coffee, he picked up his fork and told me between bites that Marty Berman had offered him some frozen halibut and salmon to take back to Seattle.

"I'll need a small cooler and ice to carry it in, so before I go to Marty's for the fish, I'd like to stop at Ulmer's and pick one up. Do you have duct tape I can use to tape it shut?"

"Does anyone in Alaska *not* have duct tape?" I asked him. "In this state, along with blue plastic tarps, it's practically building material, as well as being used for a hundred other things folks outside never even heard of. What color do you want? I have several."

We had a good day, enjoying each other's company with no further mention of Joe's relationship with Sharon and the possibility of her moving to Portland. He was cheerfully upbeat, joking with the clerk at Ulmer's Drug and Hardware who sold him a cooler for the fish, tooting the car horn and waving to another friend from high school that we passed on our way to Andy's bookstore, where he found a book he'd been wanting to read again and couldn't locate in Seattle. We had lunch at Café Cups, where we chanced upon Lew and joined him for an hour of great food and conversation, stopped at Joyce and Marty's, then took Stretch for a walk on a beach close to town. In a quick stop at the grocery, we picked up another loaf of French bread to accompany the last of the stew left over from the night before.

I drove Joe to the airport in the early evening dark so he could take the seven o'clock hop to Anchorage in order to catch his flight to Seattle. It would put him into Seattle late that evening, but he was used to that, as he did it a couple of times a year.

"Thanks, Mom—for *everything*," he said in my ear as he gave me a huge hug. "I'll let you know how it goes."

"Give Sharon my love."

"I most assuredly will."

I returned his wave as he carried his bag and the cooler out the door and onto the plane that was waiting on the tarmac for the first leg of his return to the big city.

Driving back alone through the Homer streets seemed oddly quiet and the house, when I reached it, extraordinarily empty.

I always miss my children after a visit, so it was not unexpected, but this time the feeling was stronger than usual. So, after a second cup of coffee and some consideration, I set myself a task I had been putting off for weeks—the thorough reorganization of a storage closet by the door that I had lost control of completely.

An hour later I had located several things I had thought were gone for good—a wrench and a screwdriver that both belonged in my toolbox in the garage, a package of paper Christmas napkins from the year before, and a chew toy I had meant to give to Stretch and forgotten. I also found a few grocery items I had replaced, then lost to the closet—several cans of cream of mushroom soup, for instance, a caramel crumb cake mix I had thought to try, and a brand-new package of hairpins that I remembered stashing there on my way out the door sometime the preceding summer, meaning to move them upstairs later. Having bought more, I now probably had enough to last me the rest of my life.

Satisfied with the effort that had allowed me to work off the disquiet I had been feeling, I emptied out the cold remains in my coffee cup and made myself a cup of tea. Then I shoveled out the ashes in the fireplace, built a cheerful new fire, tuned the radio softly to a favorite classical station as background company, and settled in my overstuffed chair to begin one of the books Lew had brought me Saturday evening.

Stretch, who had been getting acquainted with the newly discovered toy, came and went to sleep at my feet—welcome company.

Aside from letting him out for a quick few minutes and making myself a sandwich later, I read the late evening away and went to bed yawning, intending to continue my cleaning spree by attacking an upstairs closet the next morning.

Some old habits remain the best and most reliable remedies for escaping the odd worrisome mood.

FIVE

SOMETIME IN THE DARK MIDDLE OF THAT NIGHT I woke to the sound of Stretch growling quietly deep in his throat, intent on something I couldn't hear, though I listened closely.

Leaning over the edge of the bed, I laid a hand on his head.

"What is it, lovie? You hear something I should know about?"

He seldom growls without reason, so I got up and, without turning on the lights, carried him to the bottom of the stairs, where I put him down.

He went immediately to focus his attention on the door, though he had stopped growling.

I followed and put my ear close to listen, but heard nothing at all.

After turning on the light that illuminates the yard and much of the driveway between the house and the street, I looked out the window over the kitchen sink, but saw nothing. All was quiet and seemingly peaceful around the house as I turned on lights, checked the deck, and looked out other windows, Stretch following closely behind.

"Silly galah. I think you must have had a nightmare," I told him. "Did that gray tomcat of the neighbors' invade your dream territory?"

I turned off the lights and we both went back to bed.

Needless to say, I slept in a bit the next morning, and it was once again Stretch who woke me just after eight thirty, this time with a whine that said he needed to go out for his morning constitutional.

I put on my robe and slippers, then took him down and opened the door wide enough to let him slip out. Then I opened it wider, for, to my surprise, on the top step lay a small, neat package wrapped in a plastic bag from the grocery store and taped closed. So much for accusing Stretch of responding to nightmares!

As I picked it up I could feel that the package had the weight and shape of books and my mind turned immediately to Lew Joiner, with whom I regularly shared them. But why would Lew stop by in the middle of the night? I wondered as I let Stretch, who had finished his business in record time, back inside. I took the package to the kitchen and used my poultry shears to cut open the taped end of the bag and pulled out the contents. On a whim I had bought the shears and not once since had I ever used them on poultry, but instead found them handy for slicing open anything packaged in paper or plastic, which I often find impossible to tear.

It was indeed books, but not from Lew. On the counter before me, held together with a rubber band, lay the two Patrick O'Brian sea stories that John Walker had mentioned picking up at Andy's Bookstore the previous Thursday—the day before I met him on the spit. Removing the rubber band, I found that between the books was a folded sheet of paper, which I opened to read the following:

Dear Maxie,

Thank you so much for making my last few days so enjoyable—for sharing your house, your friends, and particularly yourself. I travel light and do not collect the books I read. So I hope you will find a place in your library for these, if you don't already have them. If you do, please give them back to Andy with my thanks.

Give Stretch a couple of pats for me.

Gratefully,
John Walker

I stood staring at the note for a long minute, then read it again.

He must have caught the Homer Stage Line bus that had left at eight thirty that morning, I decided. Why else would he have walked over from the Driftwood Inn during the night to quietly deliver the books to my front step, not realizing how sharp Stretch's hearing was when it involved his home ground? I wondered why he would have walked all the way across town and back again in the cold when he could have left the books at the hotel in my name. But maybe he had taken a taxi.

I found myself a little disappointed that he was gone, thinking he would have fit well into our relaxed and casual small-town population. I wondered briefly where he was headed after he reached Anchorage at the end of the trip. But it really didn't matter and it was highly unlikely that I would ever hear from or about him again.

I couldn't have known just how wrong I was!

It was after ten o'clock by the time I had showered and dressed for the day, fed Stretch, and eaten my own breakfast. I was about to head upstairs to start on that closet when the phone rang.

"Good morning," I answered it cheerfully, half expecting it to be Joe letting me know he had made it home.

There was a slight hesitation. Then a woman's voice spoke in my ear.

"Mrs. McNabb?"

"Yes."

"This is Julia at the Driftwood Inn. Did you know a John Walker who was staying here? He mentioned your name."

"Yes," I told her. "I met him on the spit when I took my dog out for a walk on the beach Friday afternoon. I gave him a ride back to town and, when he said he would be staying over the weekend, invited him for dinner on Saturday, with a group of friends and neighbors."

"So you didn't know him before that? Do you know where he was from?"

"He never mentioned it, seemed a little reticent, so I didn't ask."

There was a hesitation of several seconds before she spoke again.

"Can you hold on a minute, Mrs. McNabb?"

"Yes, of course, Julia."

I waited, listening intently, but she evidently covered the receiver with her hand, for all I could hear was indistinct mumbling from the other end of the line. Then a man's voice spoke in my ear.

"Mrs. McNabb?"

"Yes."

"This is State Trooper Alan Nelson. I'd like to speak with you about Mr. Walker. Could you possibly come here to the Driftwood Inn?"

"What's this about?" I asked, slightly perplexed.

"I'd rather fill you in when you get here," he told me. "At the moment I can't leave or I would come to you. Will you come?"

"Yes, of course," I told him. "I'll be there shortly."

Hearing the receiver replaced on the other end of the line, I hung up, too, wondering what could possibly have inspired the call with its request for my presence. Julia's voice had sounded a bit strained as I thought about it, so something must be amiss, especially with law enforcement involved. But how could it include John Walker?

Though we have local police, the Alaska state troopers for our part of the state are based in Anchor Point, so they must drive almost twenty miles when their presence is required in Homer. This was clearly one of those times, unless Trooper Nelson had been in our town for some other reason—a not-impossible situation. Still, it must be fairly important for him to be calling me in search of information.

"Well, so much for the closet," I told Stretch, who had en-sconced himself comfortably on the throw rug before the fireplace, in which I had earlier started a small fire to take the night's chill from the house. "I wonder what could bring the law to find out what I know—and don't know—about John Walker. He certainly didn't seem like much of a lawbreaker, but I suppose you can't always tell, can you? Still, I doubt it's anything too serious."

Considering, I readied myself for the drive into town, took Stretch to the car, and was on the road in less than ten minutes. On the passenger seat below Stretch's basket I put the two books and the note John had left on my doorstep. Though I wasn't sure just why, I had picked them up at the last minute. Something about the wording of that note had given me an uneasy feeling, especially the first line he had written: *Thank you so much for making my last few days so enjoyable—for sharing your house, your friends, and particularly yourself.*

It reminded me of what he had said the day I met him on the spit when, at the Driftwood Inn, he had come around the car to the driver's window and thanked me for the ride. Then he had said, *Maybe I'll decide to spend what's left of my life at the end of the road,* and that I had thought it was an odd way of telling me he liked Homer.

Giving myself a mental shake, I quit speculating and concen-trated instead on my driving. Evidently I would soon find out what was amiss. I pulled up outside the inn and parked beside the marked car State Trooper Alan Nelson had obviously driven, left Stretch in his basket, and went to the front door, taking the books and the note with me.

As its tinkling bell announced my presence, both Julia Bennet, the owner of the Driftwood Inn, and State Trooper Alan Nelson looked up from the table at which they were sitting.

"Mrs. McNabb?" he questioned, rising and holding out a hand to shake mine as I affirmed my identity.

He was a tall, slender man who looked about the age of my son, Joe.

"Thank you for coming," he said.

Julia brought me a cup of coffee and we all settled at a round table by a front window of the office area. Officer Nelson's hat, gloves, and clipboard lay in front of him by his coffee cup.

"I understand from the woman at the hotel that you *knew* Mr. John Walker," he said, with a glance at the report form on the clipboard.

"Well," I told him, wondering at his past tense use of the word, "I can't say I really knew him. I met him by chance last Friday, out on the spit, and gave him a lift back into town when it started to rain. At my invitation he came to my house for dinner on Saturday night, with a group of friends and my son, Joe, who was visiting from Seattle."

"So you hadn't known him before last Friday?"

"No, but he seemed a nice sort of person, with a congenial sense of humor, and fit in easily with the group on Saturday evening."

"Who was there? I may need to talk with them as well."

I gave him the names of the group and he wrote them down: Joyce and Marty Berman, Harriet Christianson, Lewis Joiner, and son Joe, who I explained had gone back to Seattle on Sunday.

"And none of them had met him before?"

"Not to my knowledge, and I think I would have known if they had."

"Well, he may have said something to one of them that would be helpful."

"Such as?"

"Did he say where he came from?"

"Not to me, but I didn't ask," I told him truthfully, then found myself thinking back to Joe's assessment of John Walker, so I told him that, too.

"My son said John was vague when asked where he was from and didn't have a regional accent. He said he was born in the South and his family lived in several places when he was young, that he had traveled a lot doing construction. He mentioned New Orleans after the hurricane, but said he had no current mailing address."

"Just where on the spit did you meet him?" Trooper Nelson questioned.

I told him and filled him in on our brief conversation.

"But he didn't tell you how he arrived here?"

"Yes, he did—said he had come down from Anchorage on the Stage Line last Wednesday and was planning to catch it back today, so he's probably almost there by now."

Julia shifted uneasily in her chair. There was a long moment of silence as Nelson frowned down at his notes on the clipboard. Then he looked up and shook his head as he spoke.

"Mrs. McNabb . . . Mr. Walker didn't take the shuttle this morning. When he didn't appear for coffee, as he usually did, about an hour later Julia says she knocked on the door to his room, but got no answer. He had paid for four nights in cash when he registered. So, assuming he had probably gone somewhere for early breakfast before catching the shuttle, she used her key and found him lying on the bed.

"Sometime, probably very early this morning, he evidently shot himself in the head with a pistol."

———————————

"Aahh . . ."

For a long moment I stared at him, unable to say a word or release the deep gasp of air I had sucked in. What he had told me just didn't make sense.

I must have lost color, for he reached across the table and laid a hand on my arm as he glanced at Julia.

"Water," he said. "Get a glass of water, will you?"

The legs of her chair shrieked on the floor as she hurriedly shoved it back, left the table, and came quickly back with a tall glass, half full.

She handed it to me and I let the second breath I had taken back out before taking a swallow. It helped.

He had leaned forward and was watching me closely and frowning in concern as I drank and set the glass on the table.

"It's okay," I told him. "I'm okay. It was the shock of what you said. You *did* mean that he's dead, didn't you?"

He nodded.

"Yes, Mrs. McNabb, I did. I'm sorry to upset you, but I need information from you if possible. Primarily, we need to know who he is and where he came from. His wallet's on a shelf next to the bed, but there's nothing in it to identify him—no papers, driver's license, credit cards—nothing at all—just two hundred and forty-three dollars in bills and a picture of a young woman. Next to the wallet is some small change—forty-six cents—and a pocketknife. Except for a few clothes in a small duffel and a small kit with a razor, a comb, and a few toiletries in the bathroom, there's nothing else."

I frowned, confused.

"But you called him by name—John Walker."

"Only because that's the name he gave when he registered here at the inn."

SIX

A COLD WIND WAS BLOWING STEADILY FROM THE WEST, catching up spray from the crests of the incoming waves of the outer inlet and hurling it onto the spit that afternoon as I walked slowly along the high edge of the shingle that had been left damp by the outgoing tide. Stretch padded along at my side, ears flopping in the breeze, shivering every so often and giving me baleful looks. Though I had insisted that he wear the red sweater I had knit for him, he was not particularly pleased at being outside instead of at home, warm and dry. The damp sand clung to his paws. He disliked it and kept shaking them frequently, to little effect.

Probably, I should have left him in the car, which I had, as usual, parked up by the road near the shops that were closed for the season, but I had wanted the company.

After a few more questions before I left the Driftwood Inn, Trooper Nelson had requested that I formally identify John Walker. So, assuring him that I had seen dead people before, having buried two husbands of my own, and would not faint, he and I had gone together to a small room near the entrance of the inn and I had sadly made the identification.

John Walker, if that really was his name, had looked peaceful enough lying on top of the carefully made bed, his head on a pillow that he had evidently covered with a towel spread over a black plastic trash bag to keep the blood from the bullet wound to his head from staining it.

"What will you do with him?" I asked as we left the room.

"His body will be sent to the lab in Anchorage," Trooper Nelson told me. "The coroner will try to establish some identification. The lack of any ID makes it seem he made an effort to conceal who he is, so it's probable that John Walker isn't his real name. Fingerprints may help us find out who he is. If he's ever had them taken they'll be on file in the national index and could help us find out where he came from, if we're lucky, but it will take some time. I'll speak to the people who were at your dinner party. They may remember something he said that could help."

I agreed and gave him the note John had left with the books.

"Interesting that he mentions the days as his *last*," he commented after he had read it.

"Yes. That struck me, too. And once, the day I met him, he said he might spend the rest of his life here in Homer. But I couldn't have known he meant anything like this."

We were standing outside John's room, facing Duggan's pub across the street.

"You know," I offered, "you might check over there. He said he might go there, and after a beer or two he may have been more forthcoming with someone—the owner, a bartender, or another customer."

"Good idea," Nelson said, nodding. "I'll try that. Thanks, Mrs. McNabb, for your assistance—and your good sense. Here's my card. Call if you have questions, or think of anything else that might be helpful."

"I will," I promised. "And could you let me know if you find out anything more about him? I'd like to know who he really was and where he came from—why he chose Homer, Alaska."

I had gone straight home, but found myself restlessly pacing from space to space inside my house, not ready to light anywhere or get back to the book I had been reading. Periodically I watched the dark clouds that were drifting in over the bay and mountains, tried to eat lunch, but found that the sandwich I made tasted more like sawdust than tuna. Finally I had given up, dressed myself and Stretch for the cold outside, and drove us out to the spit where I had first met John.

I thought it all through again as I walked the beach that miserable afternoon. What a strange thing for someone to do, leaving so many questions unanswered. If I ever decided to do away with myself, which I had no intention of doing, I thought I might decide to hike off into the wilderness that makes up the largest part of Alaska and select a place where no one would ever find or have to deal with me—or even think of looking, for that matter. Not that I really ever would, but . . .

Part of me wished I had taken my Winnebago south for the winter, as I had done the last year or two. If I had I could have avoided all this and never even met John Walker. Though he had been pleasant enough company, it had upset me deeply to think of his dying alone and in that manner. What, I wondered, could possibly have inspired it?

Kicking a piece of driftwood out of my way, I suddenly knew I was not only sad, I was angry—felt somehow used and abandoned, as if he had had some kind of obligation to me and had declined to honor it. What could have inspired that feeling? Just being kind to someone confers no debt—or shouldn't. Nevertheless . . .

I realized that I wanted answers and had been given none—probably would never get any, for who but John had them to give? And he had, by his personal reserve and his actions, refused. His suicide was clearly the most final rejection of all.

That idea depressed me all over again.

Having slowed considerably as I thought about it, I suddenly became aware that I was walking alone. Turning, I looked back to find that Stretch, unable to get my attention with his shivers and a whine or two, had simply given up and stopped several yards away. He was sitting down, staring after me, waiting to see just how long it would take for me to understand that this rebellion was serious and he wanted this miserable outing to end—now.

I had to smile. When Stretch decides to look pitiful, there is no dog I know that has perfected the art quite so successfully. He simply droops from nose to tail, cocks his head, stares at you with those irresistible liquid brown eyes, and waits to see what reaction will be forthcoming, knowing full well he'll win sympathy at the very least.

He did, of course, and I was ready enough to head for home

before the oncoming storm broke, as it was threatening to do with a few fat drops of rain that spattered dimples in the sand. Tired, unhappy, and rejected I might be, but soaking wet was a condition I could avoid. I clipped on his leash and headed toward an upward path that would take us closest to where I had parked my car.

Having his way, Stretch spared no time in climbing the bank, but once at the top he hesitated, then turned off the path and onto the wide porch in front of one of the closed shops. At first I thought he simply wanted off the damp sand that clung to his paws, but he headed straight on toward a picnic table, which I recognized as the one where John Walker had been sitting when we met him. Without hesitating he vanished under it.

"Come out from under there, you silly galah," I told him, which had no effect, so I tugged on his leash. There was still no resulting appearance and I could hear him pawing at something on the wood of the deck. Consequently, I bent to peer under the table to see what had attracted his undivided attention.

"Look," I told him, "I'm a fair bit bigger than you are, and while this may be shelter for you, it is not for me. What have you got there? Whatever it is, let it alone and come along to the car."

Curiosity to see what he was so determined to retrieve then got the better of me, so I dropped to my knees and leaned as far under the table as I could, banging my head in the process.

He was determinedly pawing at a thing that was caught in a crack between two planks of the decking—something metallic. He hesitated and looked around, clearly wanting me to salvage whatever it was.

I reached and felt a piece of cold metal.

Carefully I worked it out of the crack and, clutching it firmly, edged myself out from under the table, Stretch now willing to follow closely.

"You are a ning-nong for sure," I told him, using one of my Daniel's pet Aussie phrases for absurd behavior.

It was now raining harder, so I merely glanced at the object I had collected and hurriedly trotted us both across the road to my car, where, with my assistance, he was soon happily ensconced in his basket and ready to roll.

I hurried around to the driver's side and climbed in quickly before examining the object I carried. It was a brass belt buckle that shone dully in the half-light—the kind that has a hook on the inside to hold it in place in one of several holes in the leather of the wearer's belt. Turning it over, I was surprised to see that the outer side bore a representation of the two towers in New York that had been destroyed by terrorists.

How odd, I thought, wondering if it could possibly have belonged to the man who had been sitting there and why, if so, he hadn't recovered it. Maybe he had not lost it, but intentionally left it, concerned that it could be a clue to where he had come from, which, from his actions and reticence, he had seemed determined to conceal.

Whatever. That notion could just as easily have occurred to me because of the current events involving John Walker—or whatever his name turned out to be—and could be examined later. It was time to get off the spit for the time being.

"Okay, lovie," I told Stretch, pulling the car back onto the road, headed for town. "I have a couple of quick stops to make on the way, but we'll be home soon, I promise."

Leaving him to stay dry inside the car, I went first to take the books back to Andy, and, though I was, as always, tempted by the hundreds of books that cram the shelves of the two floors of his cozy bookstore, I resisted and left quickly without telling him about John's death—simply not ready to talk about it or answer the questions I knew he would ask.

My second stop was the liquor store, since I was almost out of whiskey after Saturday's party and decided I should pick up a couple of bottles of wine as well.

The wine I found easily near the front of the store. I put three bottles in the cart I was pushing, then went down an aisle to look for my usual whiskey, deciding also to pick up a bottle of Canadian Mist, a favorite of Becky's, who dropped in to chat from time to time. Reaching toward an upper shelf for my desired Jim Beam, I suddenly froze, noticing that near it stood a bottle of Johnnie Walker. I stood staring at it, lacking both thought and breath, as if a ghost had suddenly appeared in front of me. The letters on the red label swam as tears unexpectedly filled my eyes.

Brushing them aside with the back of my hand, I looked again. *Johnnie Walker* . . . John Walker! So that was why I had felt the name was somehow familiar on our meeting that day on the spit. It was probably just coincidence, but was there no escape from the manner and tragedy of his death?

Collecting the bottle I had been reaching for, I noticed that it too carried what could be, and probably was, a man's name—Jim Beam. How many similar labels carried the names of those proudly responsible for their distilling?

My curiosity aroused, I started along the aisle, checking out the bottles of whiskey. It soon became a rather extensive list. Besides my

Jim Beam and the bottle of Johnnie Walker that had caught my attention, I found whiskey called Jack Daniel's, Austin Nichols, W. L. Weller, Evan Williams, Elmer T. Lee, George Dickel, Elijah Craig, and even one named for Sam Houston.

From the information proudly displayed on the labels, all had been distilled in either Kentucky or Tennessee—both states that were part of the South, where John had told my son, Joe, he had been born. It made a sort of sense that he had might have selected a pseudonym from where he had originated, if that were true—and if it really was a pseudonym, as I couldn't help suspecting.

I retrieved from my purse the notebook and pen I use to make grocery lists and quickly wrote down the names I had found on the whiskey bottles, thinking that they might interest Trooper Nelson. It might possibly be, I supposed, that some of the other names might have been used for the same purpose—worth a thought at least.

By the time I left the liquor store it was pouring rain that fell almost sideways in the wind that was blowing out of the west and would probably turn to snow before nightfall. I was glad to reach home, carry in Stretch and the bottles in two trips, shake out my wet coat, and settle in for the rest of the day. With early darkness in the Alaskan far north and the addition of the clouds that had swept in, it was already time to turn on the lights.

I wanted a fire to remove the chill that had crept in as we entered, though my furnace works very efficiently, thanks to my dear Daniel, who insisted that the old one be replaced a year or two before he passed on. But besides warmth there is something consoling about having a wood fire crackling cheerfully in the corner fireplace, so I make sure to order up a full winter's supply of good dry wood each fall. I soon had the logs laid and lit and was ready to appreciate the comfort of my favorite recliner nearby.

After a snack and a long drink of water, Stretch had gone almost immediately to curl up for a nap on the hearth rug, which he assumes belongs to him. With a snoozing dog as inspiration, in the warmth of the fire I was soon nodding over my book, finally gave up, laid it down, leaned back, and followed his example.

SEVEN

MORE THAN AN HOUR LATER the ringing of the telephone brought both me and Stretch back to consciousness.

He sat up and yawned.

I got up and crossed the room to answer its summons.

"Hello."

"Hi, Mom. It's me—Joe," my son informed me, as if I wouldn't recognize his voice.

"I hear that," I told him. "So you made it home okay."

"Oh, sure. Meant to call you, but Sharon and I got into a conversation that lasted pretty late in the evening, so I decided to wait until today to tell you the news."

"So—from the sound of your voice I assume it's good and you've settled some things?"

"Yes, all good. We've—ah . . ."

I could hear him take a deep breath, then . . .

". . . decided to get married."

"Oh, Joe, I'm really happy for you both. When?"

"Well, not right away. We're thinking next spring—after we get everything settled about our work."

"So Sharon's not going to Portland?"

"No, she's still going—we're *both* going."

"Both?"

"Yes."

My son works in forensics in a Seattle crime lab, is very good at what he does, and loves his job. The idea of his giving it up filled me with concern that I immediately expressed.

"Oh, Joe. Are you sure you should give up what you like so much and are so good at? What will you do in Oregon?"

"Well, here's the good part. I spoke with the lab director this morning and, as it happens, we've been talking about working more closely with the lab in Portland, so our director has arranged for me to trade places for the winter with a guy down there. It'll be temporary. We'll establish better communication and coordination. And, best of all, I'll have my job back here in the spring. Everybody wins!"

"What about your apartment? Will you have to give it up?"

"Nope. Jacob is single and lives in downtown Portland, near where Sharon will be working, so we'll trade apartments as well as jobs—both paying our usual rent, since ours is a bit more than his."

He sounded so pleased with himself and their plans that I couldn't help being happy for them as well.

"It sounds perfect," I told him. "Now—about a wedding next year."

"Well, we've only decided one thing so far. You know that Sharon's parents are both dead and she was an only child. So, we'd like to get married up there, if that would be okay with you. We'll keep it small and informal, so it won't require too much planning and preparation."

It would indeed be more than okay with me! And I told him so with delight.

"There'll be lots of time to plan and get things ready after you get moved. Sharon and I will put our heads together when you come for Christmas. You are still coming, aren't you? When are you leaving for Oregon?"

"Yes, of course we're coming. And we're moving to Portland in a couple of weeks. Now—what's going on with you and Homer?"

For a moment I couldn't think of what to say.

"Hey, Mom. You okay?" Joe asked, sounding anxious.

"Yes, I'm fine. But the day has been—well, not the best I ever had."

"What do you mean? What's going on?"

So I told him all about John Walker's suicide, my meeting with Trooper Nelson at the Driftwood Inn, identifying John, and finding the names on the bottles of whiskey.

"He'll probably call you. I gave him the names and phone numbers of everyone who was here for dinner that night."

"I haven't anything much to tell him," Joe said. "Walker was pretty reticent about his background, if you remember my telling you."

We talked for a little longer and he promised to have Sharon call me when she had time.

I had no more than hung up the phone when there was a knock at the door.

I was surprised to find Trooper Nelson on the doorstep, his shoulders and hat covered with white flakes that were falling through the evening dark.

It was snowing, as I had expected it might.

"Come in," I invited, opening the door wide for him to step through.

"You left a message for me," he said as he brushed at his coat and hat. "Thought I'd stop and find out why before heading back to Anchor Point. You think of something else I should know?"

"Two things," I told him. "More odd ideas, maybe. Though it's more than a little speculation on my part. Take off your coat and I'll get you some coffee before I show you."

He shed and hung it with his hat on one of the hooks by the door for that purpose.

"Coffee would be welcome, thanks. Black, please."

I filled a mug and took it to the table next to the kitchen, where he came and sat across from me, laying down the clipboard he was once again carrying to reach down and give a pat to Stretch, who had come to check out this interesting stranger before giving his approval. The pat and a rub behind his ears were enough to allow that.

"What's his name?" he asked.

"Stretch."

He grinned, as people usually do.

"Great name. Now, what ideas have you had?"

First I handed him the list of names I had collected and told him about finding them on the whiskey bottles at the liquor store.

"It's just an idea. But if, not wanting to use his real name, he took John Walker from the Johnnie Walker label, might he not have used others as well—especially these that are all distilled in Tennessee and Kentucky—the South, where he told my son he was born?"

Trooper Nelson scanned the list with a frown, shook his head thoughtfully, laid it down, and gave me a long look. Then he smiled ruefully.

"Interesting idea. Ever consider going into law enforcement, Mrs. . . . ah . . . Maxie?"

"No, I never have. This was just serendipity. If I hadn't stopped to refill my liquor supply . . ."

"You had the sense to put two and two together. Whether or not it makes four, we have no way of knowing right now, but it's a possibility. I'll put it in the file and consider. Other names would be hard to check, not knowing where he's been before he came here and which ones he might have used. But nevertheless . . ."

"Another string for the bow," I suggested.

"Yes, and we haven't much to go on, have we?"

I liked the sound of that *we*. It meant he was taking me seriously.

He hesitated thoughtfully for a few moments, reading the list again, then turned it over and wrote on the back before handing it back across the table. "Here's another thing I think will interest you. When he registered at the Driftwood Inn, he wrote his name in their book like this."

John E. Walker, he had written. I stared at it, astonished.

Trooper Nelson nodded.

"Interesting, isn't it? Now, you said you had two things?"

I handed him the belt buckle we had found under the table on the spit.

"You can thank Stretch for this one," I told him, and related our under-the-table experience.

"I have no idea if it belonged to John, but it was *there*, between two planks of the deck, under the table where he was sitting when I met him."

"Another interesting possible clue," he said, turning the buckle over in his fingers to examine it. "A lot of this kind of thing was sold after that tragedy, and in lots of places, even on the West Coast. Even if it did belong to him, he could have picked it up almost anywhere, but I'll put it with the information on why and where it came from. Anything else?"

I shook my head.

He nodded, smiled again, and got up, ready to leave.

"The names are particularly worthy of note. Julia didn't catch it and neither did I until you made it clear. So, you see, I mean it when I say that if you think of anything else that might be helpful, call me. Even little things can make a difference. And you probably saw as much of him as anyone here—and paid more attention. There may be something else you'll remember," he said, putting on his coat and hat at the door.

I promised to do that and he was soon gone, having copied the names on my list into the report on his clipboard and given Stretch a last pat at the door.

From the window over the kitchen sink I watched him back his car out of the drive, noticing that there was at least an inch of snow on the ground and more was falling to blanket it, silently now that the wind had died.

Winter had, indeed, come to Homer, putting an end to most of my walks on the spit and reminding me to call the neighbor who plows the snow from my driveway with his Bobcat when necessary. Perhaps I wouldn't with this first snowfall, but I surely would soon. Still, for some reason, this year as I watched the snow fall for a moment or two, I felt that winter was closing in on me, limiting my options. Perhaps I should have gone south, but it was too late now, as I had no inclination to drive the Alaska Highway in winter weather.

In compensation, I put more wood on the dying fire and turned on the television to watch the evening news.

EIGHT

THE NEXT MORNING THE TEMPERATURE HAD RISEN as the sun came out and was melting the inch or so of snow into slush and water that ran in small creeks or formed puddles in the low spots in my drive. Even those soon disappeared.

By the time I was up and dressed for the day most of the white stuff was gone, but I knew it would soon be back and winter was definitely on the way.

Before going up to finally start sorting out the upstairs closet, I was sitting at the table with a second cup of coffee, making a list of things that my house and car would need in preparation for the approaching winter—summer tires swapped for studded winter ones, for instance—when there was a knock at my door. I opened it to find Lew Joiner on the step with a couple of books in hand.

While he hung up his coat on a hook by the door I poured him a cup of coffee and took it to the table, where he had laid down the books and found himself a chair across from where I had been sitting.

"Brought you another book on the revolution," he told me, handing one across the table. "David McCullough's new one—*1776*. It's terrific!"

"Oh, good. I've been wanting to read it. Thanks, Lew," I told him. "What's the other?"

He slid a larger book across the table as he gave me the title, "*Great American Documents*. This one's got everything from the Mayflower Compact and the Declaration of Independence to . . . well, how long has it been since you read the Constitution and the Bill of Rights?"

I shook my head.

"A very long time, I'm afraid," I told him.

"Well, I've got copies of both the Constitution and the Bill of Rights if you want to read them. You can take your time. There's no rush, but I gotta have these two back when you finish 'em. Both are bound for my permanent collection."

Lew's small house could be a bookstore. It's so full of books it reminds me of one. When I'm looking for something Andy doesn't have on hand, Lew is my go-to guy.

"Of course," I told him, and, seeing that he had half finished his coffee, fetched him a refill.

"Now," he said, changing the subject as I sat back down at the table. "What's all this about that Walker fellow doing away with himself at the Driftwood Inn? It *is* the same guy who was here Saturday night at your party, right?"

I should have known that the details of John's death would spread through our small town like wildfire. There is always gossip circulating, especially in the winter, when the tourists disappear, things slow down, and there's not much that's exciting going on.

"Yes," I told him with a sigh. "I'm sorry to say it is. But I don't know why. Where did you hear about it?"

"From my cousin, Caroline Harrison, who got it from her daughter, Julia Bennet. You know, she was a Harrison before she married Jess Bennet's oldest boy, Bob."

Sometimes it seems that the permanent population of Homer is all related one way or another, although in the last few years there has been an influx of new, retired people buying or building homes and summer cottages on the bluff above town. Still, many of the names are well known and can be traced back to our earliest settlers in the area, like the Harrisons and the Bennets.

I told Lew why he would probably soon have a visit from Trooper Nelson and about finding John's name on the whiskey bottle, figuring I might as well. He would hear it somewhere soon anyway.

"John Walker. Johnnie Walker," he tried them both out, then frowned and shook his head. "It *must* have been a pseudonym. Who in their right mind would name a child after a bottle of booze?"

Who indeed? I wondered after Lew had departed, but was convinced that John had selected his own name—or pseudonym.

After that my phone just about rang itself off the line with people calling to ask questions. News, good or bad, spreads like lightning in a town as small as Homer. After a while I considered leaving it for the machine to answer, but was afraid people would simply come rapping on my door with their curiosity if I did. And I had passed the point of tolerance in relating the story another time. It simply made me sad.

So I didn't respond to the knock on the door that I heard from upstairs, where I had retreated to attack the closet.

I only lock my door at night, or if I leave the house, so I wasn't surprised when I heard the door open and close behind the person who had knocked. Then Harriet Christianson—who knows she's always welcome—called my name from the bottom of the stairs.

"Maxie? Are you up there?"

"Certainly am," I replied, stepping down from the stool on which I was standing to reach the top shelf. "Don't bother to come up, I'll be right down."

When I arrived at the bottom of the stairs I found that she had removed her coat and was standing at the kitchen counter to open a bottle of Merlot. She turned and smiled.

"Aren't you supposed to be at the library?" I asked.

"So—I took an afternoon off. Things were slow at the moment, so I skipped out.

"I figured you've probably been run ragged with a hundred questions about that Walker guy," she went on. "Don't worry. I don't intend to ask you any more, having already heard several versions of the thing from people who have nothing but rumors to go on.

"If you'll get some glasses, we'll smooth your ragged edges with a bit of good wine."

"Oh, you are an angel," I told her, getting two of my best wineglasses from the upper cupboard. "You have no idea how welcome you are, with or without the libation—but right now I'm gladdest to see you with it. Even Stretch knows you're welcome—never barks when he knows it's you."

We took our glasses and the bottle across the room to sit comfortably on opposite ends of the sofa, Stretch padding along after us to lie down again on the hearth rug.

"Here's to better days," Harriet said, reaching to clink glasses with me.

"I certainly agree with that," I told her.

"I figured you were fed up with calls when I got a busy signal twice, then your answering machine," she told me. "But I decided you were most likely hiding out instead."

"You know me too well," I said, and laughed. "That's exactly what I've been doing, and what you'd do as well, I suspect."

"Right you are. Did you notice that the snow on the mountains across the bay isn't termination dust anymore? It's all the way down now, thanks to yesterday's storm."

"I did notice. But I'm glad it's warm enough to melt most of it here in town. We'll have more soon anyway."

She nodded. "I saw your list on the table, including a tire change. I was going to take my car in to have its winter ones put on, but the place was mobbed. So I went to the liquor store for the wine instead. The roads won't be slick for a while yet, so my old Galloping Gertie can wait a few days for studded shoes."

"You're right, but . . . ," I told her, then hesitated a moment before going on. "While cleaning out my upstairs closet I was thinking that I might run away from home for a day or two, go to Anchorage—do some Christmas shopping."

"Sounds like a good idea," she agreed. "I'd love to go with you if I didn't have to work. Are Joe and Sharon still planning to come for Christmas?"

"Oh, yes. And you'll be glad to hear that they've solved the problem of living in two cities in different states by *both* moving to Portland, at least temporarily. Joe's already lined up a forensics job there. They're going to wait to get married until next spring. And they want to do it up here."

"Terrific. I figured Joe would get his act together and work it all out somehow. I'm really happy for them."

"So am I. They're not churchgoing sorts, so they'll want something small and informal, and this house isn't big enough. Got any ideas?"

"Well—you might ask Becky about Niqa Island. You know my niece was married out there and it was great. People came across the bay in their boats or by water taxi. The ceremony and reception could be on that big deck at her sister Gretchen's lodge above the east cove, or inside if it rained. She's set up for numerous guests, if they wanted to stay over, but most of Joe's friends here probably have their own boats and would go back to town instead."

"That would be perfect," I told her. "I'll ask Becky about it. Joe said Sharon would call me soon, so I'll suggest it to her, but I know they'll agree that would be grand."

"The two of them could stay in Mark's tree house. I'm sure he'd be happy to loan it."

A number of years earlier, Mark, an Anchorage-based architect and family friend, had built a spectacular tree house high above the west beach of the island between three huge spruce trees and periodically loaned it out to friends when he wasn't using it himself. It added to the limited amount of space available in the original houses that had been built on both south-facing coves through the years after the family homesteaded on the island across Kachemak Bay from Homer. The rest of the island was BLM land, so no one else could build or live there.

"I'll ask, but I know they'd love it," I responded to both Harriet's suggestions.

We ignored the phone and let the answering machine take care of calls while we chatted for the rest of the afternoon, making plans I could offer Joe and Sharon when they had moved successfully and things slowed down for them. I knew Sharon would call and it was nice to have options to offer for the following spring.

I made sandwiches and heated soup for a casual dinner. We finished the wine and it was close to seven o'clock when Harriet left, with the admonition not to let the telephone make me crazy.

"Thanks for coming," I told her as I hugged her good-bye. "I feel much better now. I'm sorry I won't be able to come to the quilting circle, but I'll make it next time."

"So you're still thinking of escaping to Anchorage?" she asked, shrugging on her coat and fishing the car keys out of a pocket.

"Yes, as a matter of fact I think I will do just that—first flight out in the morning. I'll call Grant Aviation, fly up, rent a car at the airport, and spend a few days shopping. That's always good therapy, yes? Maybe I'll drive out and see Alex Jensen and Jessie Arnold. Joe will want to invite them to the wedding, so I'll give them a heads-up to expect it in the spring."

"All good ideas," Harriet agreed. "Call me when you get back."

"I'll do that."

NINE

At nine o'clock Wednesday morning I was aboard the plane in which Grant Aviation would fly me to Anchorage, feeling like the runaway that I, of course, was. There was, however, little guilt involved in my escape, but rather a distinct sense of relief.

Stretch went along, snug in his carrier behind the rear seat I had taken to keep an eye on him. Used to the carrier, he would be content to take a nap for most of the just-under-an-hour flight.

As we taxied down the runway for takeoff I glanced around at my fellow passengers.

There were six, half filling the plane.

Three were obviously businessmen, dressed in suits and ties and carrying briefcases.

A young couple sat together holding hands in seats just behind the pilot. I recognized the girl, as I knew her mother from quilting club and remembered that I had seen her wedding picture in a local newspaper several months earlier.

There was one other woman sitting halfway up the small plane on the opposite side. I had guessed that, probably, she was not a Homer resident, for I had seen her in the waiting room before boarding looking through the brochures that filled a rack on the wall with information on Homer and the surrounding area. As I watched she had collected a few that she tucked into the large shoulder bag she carried and, now aboard the plane, she was studying one I recognized as containing a map of the spit and its various offices and businesses. We have few tourist visitors to Homer so late in the year and I wondered briefly what had brought her there, but people do come and go for all kinds of reasons.

As we had approached the plane, with a hand motion she had offered to let me board in front of her, but knowing I wanted a rear seat I had thanked her and waited until last.

Though there were a few clouds, it was mostly clear and sunny as we flew northeast over the Kenai Peninsula. I was able to see the lakes, large and small, as they passed beneath us. Knee-deep in one of the small ones a moose and her half-grown calf were browsing on the reeds and pondweed that were still scantily available at its thinly frozen edge. During the winter when the ponds freeze solid and the snow is deep, the huge ungulates rely on the needlelike leaves of conifers for the up to forty pounds of food they need each day.

Though much of the peninsula is a national wildlife refuge and is full of moose, I saw no more from the air that morning and we were soon passing over Cook Inlet headed for the Anchorage airport.

Where the inlet divides, Anchorage occupies a projection of land between it and the Chugach Mountains to the east. The northern waters become the smaller Knik Arm and the southern, Turnagain Arm, so named in different languages by at least three captains of sailing ships, including Captain Cook, who was searching for a northwest passage from the Pacific to the Atlantic. All, however, were disappointed in their quests and had to turn back into the Pacific, thus the name.

On sunny days I always love flying between Anchorage and Homer because, besides the inlet and its arms, several mountain ranges are often visible from the air, all beautiful at any time of year.

By the time we landed I was ready to collect the rental car I had called ahead to reserve and Stretch and I were soon headed for downtown Anchorage, where I had booked a room at the Hilton Hotel and asked for one high on the north-facing side. From there, I had found that if I woke early on a clear day I could watch the rising sun cast a rosy glow over both Mount McKinley and Mount Foraker, the rest of the Alaska Range, and Mount Susitna farther west. It was a grand view, but usually hidden in clouds. Still, it was worth a chance.

Leaving the rental car to be parked by one of the hotel staff, I checked in and Stretch and I went up to our room to leave the necessaries I had brought along for the two of us. I let him out of the carrier, gave him water, and put him on his leash and myself into my coat, and we were off for a day of shopping and enjoying the downtown section of Alaska's largest city.

Going through the lobby on our way out I was surprised to see the woman from the plane sitting in a chair to one side of the elevators. As we headed for a side door, she looked up over the top of the *Homer News* that she was reading, but gave no indication that she recognized me, her attention on Stretch, who had been out of sight in his carrier when we boarded and disembarked. I would have smiled and nodded as we passed, but she had already returned to her reading and didn't seem to notice. As I held the door for Stretch to exit in front of me, however, I glanced back and found her watching us leave.

Outside, I was glad to see, as I had noticed driving in from the airport, that the streets and sidewalks were bare of snow. We walked up to Fifth, then turned east for half a block to Penney's department store, which forms the west end of a large downtown mall that connects to numerous tempting shops on several levels, none of which we have in Homer.

I had a great time perusing the offerings of a number of stores and shops for a couple of hours, then, after a sandwich lunch at a table in the upper food court, decided to leave the mall and head for Title Wave, a bookstore across the street. There I spent more than an hour and added three books to my purchases, one on the Revolutionary War that I was almost sure Lew didn't have and knew I hadn't read.

It was well into the afternoon when we finally returned to the hotel. I had a nap in mind before dinner and knew that Stretch would be ready for one as well. He is a welcome and patient travel companion, interested in just about everything he sees, but he tires faster than I do, his short legs a blur of motion in keeping up with anything but a casual stroll.

Though my shopping, for Christmas and in general, had gone well, I was ready to give it up for the time being and settle in with my new books. I had found a warm sweater for Sharon in a luscious shade of peach, a couple of old favorite movies on DVD for Joe, and a few other small gifts for friends and family.

The message light on the telephone was blinking demandingly when we came through the door to our room.

Oh, no! I thought, assuming that someone else with questions concerning John Walker had somehow tracked me down. After putting my purchases on the bed I would not be using, I shrugged off my coat, kicked off my shoes, and sat down to check the message—or messages, as the case might prove to be.

I was relieved to hear Jessie Arnold's recorded voice instead, requesting that I call her back at home, and did so immediately.

I had talked to her the evening before, but we had not decided on a time to get together for a visit, though she had invited me to come and stay with them for a day or two before I headed back to Homer.

Jessie and her significant other, Alex Jensen, have become two of the best friends I have, whose company I don't have the chance to enjoy often enough. They live together outside Wasilla, which is about forty miles east of Anchorage, off the Parks Highway, which winds its way north to Fairbanks, passing Denali Park about halfway.

Jessie is a musher of sled dogs, and keeps and trains a large kennel of them in the yard next to the comfortable log cabin she had constructed there a number of years ago after the original burned.

Alex is an Alaska state trooper with the detachment in Palmer, another Matanuska Valley town a few miles east of Wasilla.

The pair met when Jessie was running a team of dogs to Nome in the famous Iditarod Trail Sled Dog Race and tangled with a killer on the trail. It wasn't long afterward that Alex moved in to live with her, and they've been together ever since.

I dialed the number and Jessie was quick to answer on the second ring, which told me she had been waiting.

"Hey, Maxie! How are you?"

"Fine—pretty much," I told her. "Some disconcerting things going on in Homer, but I'm fine and simply playing hooky from a few unwelcome phone calls and questions I'll tell you about later."

"Well," she said, "I was hoping you'd take time from shopping to call this afternoon. The Caswells have invited us for bridge tonight, so I wanted to talk to you before we went out for the evening and make sure you were coming to stay with us tomorrow as planned."

"We'd love to, if it's not interrupting anything for you."

"Not at all," she told me. "I'm assuming from that *we* that you brought Stretch. But you know me this time of year. There's not enough snow to run sleds and dogs on, so I keep wandering around the lot, keeping an eye on the sky—which has remained sunny, dammit!—and hearing how you're getting snow in Homer. I'd more than welcome you if only as a distraction. But you know you're much more than that and are welcome here anytime.

"And I can't forget to tell you that Alex agrees and is looking forward to your arrival. You did bring Stretch, didn't you? Tank wants to know."

I heard the grin in her voice and assured her I was accompanied by my usual canine companion, who had become firm friends with Jessie's lead dog, Tank.

"I've got a little more shopping to attend to out at the Diamond Center, but will drive in your direction tomorrow—arrive midafternoon, if that works for you."

It did and we ended the call, knowing there would be plenty of time for conversation in the next couple of days.

Running away from home is sometimes best when you can avoid telling anyone just where you are going. That was exactly what I had done, except for Jessie, and, to my great satisfaction, my phone didn't ring once that evening, nor did anyone knock on my door.

Leaving Stretch in the room, I had gone downstairs for dinner after watching the news on television. After dinner I watched an old favorite movie on television, went to bed early, and slept well and dreamlessly.

The next morning I got up early to take Stretch for a quick walk, knowing he would need to be taken out for his morning constitutional. It was still dark outside and cold, so we didn't stay put long and were soon back in our room, where I ordered breakfast, fed him, and, while I waited for my meal, read the *Anchorage Daily News*, which I had found outside my door. A glance out the window had shown me that the whole sky was overcast, so there was no sunshine to gild the faraway mountains to the north, which were so tall they were hidden in the clouds. This was more often than not the case, with Mount McKinley the highest mountain in North America. I guess we are lucky that we see it at all from Anchorage, considering how far away it is. Ah, well—one can't have everything, can one?

The coffee that arrived swiftly was good and strong, the eggs

Benedict and toast tasty and still warm under their metal cover. So I took my time eating, and by the time it was growing light outside I was ready to dress, pack up what little I had removed from my small suitcase, and head for the Diamond Center, another mall across town.

TEN

AFTER ENJOYING A LITTLE MORE LEISURELY SHOPPING and lunch at the Diamond Center south of downtown Anchorage, I drove out the Glenn Highway toward Palmer, turned left just before reaching it, and was soon in Wasilla, a smaller community north of Palmer. Taking the road that angled west I had soon driven just over ten miles to where Jessie lived and was expecting me.

She must have been watching when I turned the rental car into her drive that Thursday afternoon and drove up to park in front of her log house at just before three. She came flying out the door, pulling on a jacket as she took the stairs from the broad front porch two at a time—somehow without falling—her sled dog Tank following more cautiously behind her. Reaching the bottom, she all but hurled herself into an enthusiastic hug for me as I stepped out of the car.

"Oh, Maxie," she told me, leaning back and giving me a grin. "I'm so glad to see you!"

"And I you," I told her.

"I feel like it's been ages since I saw you last."

"Well, it hasn't been that long actually. I was here just after the earthquake."

"That's right, you were, but it feels like longer ago. I just wish we lived closer together—either you here, or us there. How long can you stay? A week? A month?"

I had to smile at her—more than welcoming, as always.

"Not anywhere near that long. But if you can put up with me and Stretch we'll stay tomorrow and Saturday, then head home on Sunday. I already have a reservation with Grant Aviation."

"Of course it's okay. What's your excuse for coming up this time?"

"Do I need one?"

"Of course not! I'm just curious, as usual, and you sounded a bit in need of an escape on the phone."

"You have no idea how right you are," I told her. "And that's exactly what I did—escape! But let's get inside where it's warm and I'll tell you all about the past few days. I'm sure you've a cup of tea for an old lady in need of it. And somewhere here in a paper bag I have a bottle of Jameson that I picked up in Anchorage."

"'Old lady'? Hardly!" Jessie scoffed. "And leave the whiskey where it is," she instructed. "You're carrying coals to Newcastle. I have a brand-new bottle waiting on the table in the house and the water's hot enough for tea, if you'd like to have both."

She helped me by lifting my small bag out of the backseat while I collected Stretch from his basket and put him on the ground so he could greet Tank, who was eagerly awaiting him with tail wagging.

Jessie's larger dog then followed close at my heels as I picked up and carried Stretch up the steps to the porch.

In just a few minutes Jessie and I were settled at her table near the kitchen with welcome shots of Jameson and an accompanying cup of tea for me, as promised. Accompanied by her sled dog, Stretch had reacquainted himself with her house by padding around the large open area that was kitchen, dining area, and living room combined. Satisfied, he lay down side by side with Tank on a colorful rug near Jessie's potbellied stove.

"Here's to lasting friendships," she said, lifting her glass.

"And the friends that treasure them," I gave back.

We sipped and Jessie leaned forward to set down her drink and rest both elbows on the table.

"Now," she requested, "tell me why you've run away from home. What's wrong?"

I hesitated and thought for a long moment before answering her.

"You know," I said finally. "If you'll wait awhile for an answer to that, I'd much rather tell it just once and I'd like Alex to hear it, too. He may have some ideas to contribute to the strange and puzzling situation I've inadvertently become part of and run away from."

"Interesting," she returned. "But wait if you want. Alex should be home soon anyway. When he heard you were coming today he decided to play hooky himself and take a couple of hours off this afternoon."

"Good. And thanks."

"No problem for me—but it sounds like you may have one."

"Sort of," I answered. "Tell me how your kennel is stacking up for racing this year. Are you going to run the Iditarod again—or the Yukon Quest?"

Less than an hour later we heard a truck in the drive, footsteps on the stairs and front porch, and someone whistling "She'll Be Comin' 'Round the Mountain When She Comes."

The door flew open and Alex Jensen appeared through it with a grin and a hearty, "Hey there! Hello-o-o, Maxie! What a treat to find you here keeping company with my favorite girl."

He leaned to give Jessie—who had risen and hurried across the room—a one-armed hug and a kiss from under his handlebar mustache, then handed her a grocery bag.

"Good to see you, too, love. Here's the stuff you wanted from the store."

"Thanks," Jessie told him, and headed for the kitchen with the bag.

After removing his coat, hat, and boots, he crossed the room sock-footed in long strides to share a hug with me as well.

"Did you come to help me solve crimes again?" he teased as he sat down at the table. "I've not got much that's really interesting just now."

"Well," I told him, "I just might have something that will pique your curiosity at least."

"Fire away," he told me, leaning forward to reach for the bottle of Killian's Jessie had brought from the refrigerator to set on the table in front of him.

"Wait a minute," she called from back in the kitchen. "I want to hear, too, and need to do a couple of things in here first."

When she came back to the table and sat down, Alex nodded in my direction. "Go ahead, Maxie. Have you been stirring up trouble in Homer, or just playing detective again?"

"Neither," I told him. "I'd much rather this thing had never landed in my lap, but . . . It all started a week ago when Stretch and I went for a walk on the spit and met a man who said he was just visiting and had hiked out from town. A storm was on its way in, so we gave him a ride back to town when it started to rain. Then . . ."

As they both listened attentively, I told them everything I could think of about John Walker, how I had met him and that he had come to dinner that Saturday night and fit in well with the group, but left son Joe wondering why he was vague about where he had come from and been doing. I related how he had left the two books on my doorstep Sunday night and that I had assumed he had caught the Homer Stage Line back to Anchorage, the phone call I had received from Trooper Alan Nelson, my subsequent visit to the Driftwood Inn, our interview and my identification of John's body. I finished with the belt buckle Stretch had found under the table on the spit, then my shock at finding his name on the whiskey bottle, and having it backed up by his way of signing the guest book at the inn.

"After that my phone rang constantly from people asking questions, and I decided to run away for a few days. So here I am and more than grateful for this port in a storm."

Alex had leaned back in his chair as I talked, a thoughtful frown lowering his brow as he listened closely until I was through.

"I know and respect Alan Nelson," he told me. "He's good at his job, so you can count on his doing it well and thoroughly. The dead man's body would have been brought up to the crime lab in Anchorage yesterday or the day before, and they may have been able to identify him by his prints, if he's ever had them taken. It's one of the first things they'll do. I can check with a phone call in the morning, if you like."

I nodded. "I'd very much like to know who he really was and where he came from."

"It's interesting that he would take a name from a brand of whiskey," Jessie said. "He must have had a sense of humor."

"If he used that one, he might have used some of the others," I told her. "I found that there's a lot of whiskey named after the people who made it."

She had also been listening intently while I told my tale and now, as she reached to pour us all another shot of Jameson, she ventured a question concerning something I wondered about, but had not really considered, given that I had no way of knowing, or finding, the answer.

"Do you suppose he might have been in New York when the towers fell and got the belt buckle there? If so, given his obvious intent to hide his identity and where he was from, it would make sense that he would get rid of it."

"That's possible, I guess. Given where and how it was found, I imagine they'll check that out as well," Alex told her. "But, as Nelson said, those buckles were probably sold nationwide and it could have come from anywhere. Hard to follow up, I'd say."

After a few more questions and speculations, Jessie called a halt to the discussion.

"Maxie's clearly had about all she needs of this right now. Let's change the subject. How are Joe and Sharon?"

I was pleased to tell them about the current temporary move to Portland and that they had decided on a wedding in the spring.

"They're coming up for Christmas, so we'll make plans then, but it's possible we'll have the ceremony on Niqa Island across the bay if Becky and her sister are agreeable. You'll come down for it, yes?"

Jessie nodded thoughtfully and a little hesitantly, then gave me a smile.

"Of course," she said. "Past experiences aside, I really like that island. It'll be good to replace old memories with pleasant new ones."

Then I remembered that before we had met she had hidden out on the island far from home, where a stalker she thought she had escaped had managed to find her anyway. But she assured me it would be fine, as I knew it truly would.

"I wouldn't miss their wedding for anything. And please tell Joe and Sharon that we'd love to see them while they're here in December, right, Alex?"

"Yes, of course we'd *like* to, but you're forgetting that we've planned to go to my mother's in Idaho for the holidays," he reminded her. "I've already put in for time off."

"You're right and I must have fluff for brains in forgetting. Give them our good wishes instead, Maxie. And tell them we'll surely be there with bells on in the spring."

"I'll make sure you get an invitation with the dates."

We had a good dinner and a pleasant evening with a little wine, soothing background music, and much laughter as we caught up on what we had all been doing since the last time we three had seen each other. As Alex had to work the next day, we made it an early evening and I fell asleep with Stretch lying comfortably on a rug next to my bed.

It was a definite relief to be away from Homer for a few days that would have been full of questions for which I had no answers. I knew Stretch was happy to be back with his old friend, Tank, who Jessie had taken out to his box in the kennel for the night.

"Can't make the rest of my guys jealous by letting him stay inside at night," she told me with a grin. "Besides, he snores sometimes— enough to wake me up. Would you believe it?"

"I would. Stretch does, too, at times. So did my Daniel, whose dog he was first. A time or two after Daniel died I found myself half awake waiting to hear that familiar sound and hearing Stretch instead."

As I drifted off I had to smile as Stretch reminded me of that fact with a couple of gentle snores, then rolled over and they stopped, or if they didn't I slept soundly enough not to hear them.

ELEVEN

I WOKE THE NEXT MORNING to the welcome scent of coffee and could hear Alex down in the kitchen, singing as he made breakfast.

Stretch was gone from his place on the braided rug next to the bed, so I knew Jessie had brought Tank inside and the two dogs were probably now downstairs and happily ensconced in their usual spot by the stove.

I rolled out of bed, washed my face, combed and pinned my hair up in its twist, and dressed comfortably for the day in slacks and a sweater, glad to find the sun shining brightly in the window. I smiled, knowing that Jessie would see it simply as another day without snow for taking her dogs out on the local trails, unless she used her four-wheeler, as many mushers did before the snow fell and grew deep enough for sleds.

"Good morning," she called, coming from the cupboard with plates to set the table as I came down the stairs.

Alex leaned around the corner of the kitchen to greet me with a grin. "Sleep well?" he asked. "Sorry if I woke you with my off-key warbling."

"Not at all. I'll take your warbling over an alarm clock any day. And I enjoy hearing it anyway."

In short order he was setting a platter full of French toast, bacon, and eggs over easy on the table between Jessie and me.

"Help yourselves to syrup or jam before it gets cold," he encouraged, reaching to fill our coffee mugs before setting the pot back in the kitchen to keep warm and coming to the table with his own mug in hand.

"I called the crime lab in Anchorage earlier," he told me between bites. "They're still at it, but so far have had no joy in finding a match to your John Walker's fingerprints. It takes a fair amount of time to search all those millions of prints, so I'll check again later, but don't hold your breath about it. I'll call if I find out anything."

He finished his breakfast in short order and was on the porch calling good-bye on his way to work a few minutes later, leaning back in before he shut the door to make a suggestion to Jessie.

"Ask Maxie if she'd like to go over to Oscar's for chili tonight. Last week he predicted that tonight would be the night, but you might call and make sure."

Oscar's was a nearby local pub that had been replaced and renamed after a fire destroyed it several years earlier. I knew that Oscar also owned a pub in town that was simply named Oscar's and had intended a different name for this one. The local people, however, had always called it Oscar's Other Place no matter what he intended, so he cheerfully gave in and put up a sign making the name official, acknowledging their feeling of ownership in having helped with the rebuilding of it.

It was frequented by many of the local sled dog racers, their handlers, and their followers, and at least once a month Oscar offered homemade chili and the place was always more crowded than usual. I had been there once before on a visit to Alex and Jessie's and was definitely agreeable to repeating the experience.

Jessie made the confirming phone call and came back to the table with a grin.

"Alex almost never forgets chili night at Oscar's. I assume you want to go?"

"You bet," I agreed. "Oscar makes better chili than anyone I know. Besides, he runs a good bar and, as you've told me, never has a bad word for anybody."

"Well—hardly ever," Jessie said, and grinned. "Just don't get him started on his feelings for the guy who burned down the old one. They aren't so good-natured and friendly."

"I wouldn't be either if someone destroyed my house," I told her. "Neither would you."

"Right. I wasn't when mine burned," she said, recalling another past arson.

Before sitting back down she poured us both more coffee and removed our now empty plates to return to the kitchen. Coming back to her place at the table, she paused to stare out the window for a few seconds, a frown on her face as she turned away.

"Rain!" she said with a sigh. "More rain! When are we going to get some snow? We had a good amount for a few days last month, but it went away as fast as it came and I only got half a dozen runs in with the mutts and sled. They're getting fat and lazy, and so is their owner at this rate."

I had to smile, for she is anything but fat or lazy, and slim as a girl. She seems almost always in motion, doing something, even if it is just walking back and forth to once again check the sky for any hint of snow-bearing clouds, as she had just done.

She smiled back and sat down to take a sip of her coffee.

"What would you like to do today?" she asked me. "You said you were shopping in Anchorage, so you're probably shopped out by now. Is there anything else you'd like to do while you're here? I should take a run into town to pick up a pile of food I ordered for the mutts and a couple of new harnesses for my leaders. Anywhere you'd like to go?"

"I wouldn't mind stopping at the bookstore in Wasilla," I told her. "You know Annabel's under the clock tower. There's a book I'd like to find for son Joe for Christmas, but it's out of print. Neither Title Wave nor C and M Books in Anchorage had a copy and it wasn't to be found in Homer. Annabel's might have it. Could you drop me there while you run your errands?"

She gave me an amused smile with her answer.

"Sure. Break my heart! Make me come into a bookstore to find you. We may both be in serious trouble with books to be had. Good thing Alex's working today. He's a bigger addict for them than I am."

We both glanced across the room at the two tall bookcases under the stairway, which were packed full of so many books that several piles had been stacked up on the floor in front of them.

"Looks familiar to me," I told her. "You've seen mine. There's not much difference."

We took Jessie's truck, as she could load it with the bags of the dog food she needed and my rented car was too small. But we left our two dogs at home, knowing the cab would be overly crowded with four of us in it, and its bed was filled with the large box used to transport her teams of dogs wherever they were needed, each in its own compartment. Tank and Stretch would be left behind and relied on to behave themselves inside the house while we were gone for a couple of hours, well trained as they were.

In less than half an hour I was waving Jessie out of the parking lot in front of Meta Rose Square, a neat building with a few shops, the tall clock tower high above, and, my goal of the moment, Annabel's.

Besides several customers, both Carol and Richard Kinney, the owners, were there and greeted me warmly when I went in. Though I seldom have a chance to talk with them and browse their shelves of new and used books, it is always a treat when I do, for they are book people to the core and instant friends of book lovers.

Wonder of wonders, they *did* have a copy of the book I wanted for Joe, a book of photos of Homer back when it was just beginning to be a town, which pleased me, as I was about to give up looking. I also found a couple of Ellis Peters mysteries I didn't have in my collection and a wonderful old book of selected verse by Edna St. Vincent Millay, a favorite poet of mine since college days.

The best part of an hour later, I was about to tackle the history shelves in search of something Lew didn't already have in his historical collection in Homer when Jessie came breezing in, greeted the Kinneys, and grinned at the pile of books I had waiting for me at the front desk.

"I had a hunch I was leaving you too long," she said. "Not fair. You got a head start. Did you find the one you were looking for?"

Assuring her I had, I was headed for books on the Revolutionary War when the cover of a paperback book displayed face-out on a shelf I was passing caught my eye:

BIG SHOTS

THE MEN BEHIND THE BOOZE

THE REAL-LIFE STORIES OF

JACK DANIEL

CAPTAIN MORGAN

JIM BEAM

AND MANY MORE

I opened it to the table of contents and found that most of the chapters listed gave the names of the men who had created the various liquors, including a fair number of whiskeys with names I had written down from the bottles on the shelves of my local liquor store. Chapter eleven was Johnnie Walker.

That was enough for me to take it to go through later and give up searching for another day, with two books I didn't think Lew had on his shelves and might enjoy adding.

Jessie came back to the front desk and I smiled to see that she had wasted no time in creating a pile of her own, which had grown almost as tall as mine in the few minutes she had taken to shelf-read.

"If we have something you're looking for and can't find, we'll be glad to mail it to you in Homer," Carol said to me. "Just give us a call."

"I'll remember that," I told her as I paid for the books, tucked their card between the pages of one of them, and thanked them for their assistance.

As we headed for the building's exit we passed a cooking shop that had intrigued me the last time I was there. I slowed and turned my head to look and Jessie laughed.

"Don't even think about it," she said, clutching my elbow and towing me toward the outer doors. "Keep saying to yourself, 'I have to *fly* home.'"

But I pulled away and went back to take another look from outside the shop's door, for as we passed I had caught a glimpse of not the terrific assortment of anything related to cooking or eating, but a figure that I thought I recognized—the woman who had been on the plane I had taken from Homer to Anchorage and in the lobby of the hotel when I passed with Stretch on my way to do some shopping two days earlier.

"What is it?" Jessie asked at my shoulder. "Something you really want to take a look at? I'm sure they do mail orders, too."

I shook my head and turned back toward the door to the outside again.

"No," I told her. "Just someone I thought I recognized, but I guess I was mistaken."

I thought about it as Jessie drove us home and somehow it made me uneasy. Was the woman somehow following me? If so, why? But it seemed unlikely that she could have been in all three of the towns I had either left or visited on this trip by accident—didn't it? Who was this woman who kept showing up in my escape from home? If she wanted something, had something to say to me, why couldn't she be direct and ask?

"That's a worried sort of frown," Jessie commented as she turned the truck off the highway into her driveway and drove up to park near the house. "You okay?"

Quickly, I relaxed the frown, which I hadn't been conscious that I was exhibiting, and gave her a smile instead. "Oh, yes, I'm fine. Want help unloading your dog food?"

"Not necessary. It's fine for the moment in the dog boxes in back. When Alex comes home he'll help get it in the shed before we head for Oscar's. Those bags are pretty heavy, and you're supposed to be company anyway, not kennel help. Let's go in and see how the mutts are doing."

"The mutts" had heard us drive in and met us at the door with tails wagging, as eager to greet us as if we had been gone a week instead of a couple of hours. They make such an odd pair in size that it always amuses me to watch them together, and this was no exception. I forgot my consideration of the woman I thought I might have seen and turned to helping make sandwiches for lunch, which we ate at the table while we looked over the books we had brought back.

The better part of an hour later I was examining the one I had found for Joe when Jessie suddenly shoved back her chair and stood up to face the window.

"*Snow!*" she crowed. "It's *snowing!*"

I turned to see that, sure enough, fat white flakes were falling like a lace curtain through the air and into the yard and had already thinly coated the roofs of the dog boxes in the yard with half an inch or so.

"Oh, I do hope it doesn't all melt off this time," she said.

It didn't, but went on coming down quite steadily for the rest of the afternoon. There were three or four inches outside by the time Alex arrived.

"Well, you got your wish finally," he said, greeting me as he swept Jessie into a hug. "About time, too. I was beginning to think you'd soon be impossible to live with, but I checked and the weatherman is predicting snow for the next twenty-four hours at least and temperatures cold enough so it won't melt off immediately this time."

"I know. I checked, too," she told him gleefully, stomping on boots and reaching for her coat. "Don't take off your parka. I've got a load of dog food that needs to go in the shed and can use some help."

I watched from the window as they went out together. Jessie skipped ahead and scooped up enough snow for a snowball, which she hurled at Alex. He instantly retaliated and the battle continued for a few minutes until he grabbed up a handful and washed her face with it.

What a great couple they made, I thought as I watched and laughed at their antics. In a few trips to the storage shed, they had unloaded the sacks of dog food, then fed and watered the dogs in the yard, and were coming back inside, shaking off the snow before entering.

"She gets like this every fall, waiting for snow. I think she'd be happy to have it year-round if the weather would cooperate," Alex told me with a grin. "Now—everyone ready to head over to Oscar's? How're you at dart tossing, Maxie?"

"Rusty, but willing," I told him.

So we were soon on our way in his larger truck with its crew cab, taking Stretch and Tank along, knowing they were always welcome at the Other Place.

TWELVE

We had a fine evening at Oscar's Other Place.

From behind the bar he greeted our two dogs and us warmly, as he set up our bottles of Killian's lager.

"Good to see you again, Maxie," he told me. "Has it snowed in Homer yet?"

"Once, but it was gone when I left a couple of days ago. There'll be more soon, according to the predictions."

He waved us toward the chili, which was set on a table across the room in a large kettle with a hot plate under it and bowls and spoons handy.

"Help yourselves. Good thing you came early. It'll be gone in another hour. Word gets out, you know?"

The place was full of local people, mostly those with kennels of sled dogs, all delighted with the snowy weather, but we found a table somehow and enjoyed the chili between greeting friends and fellow mushers of Jessie's. As soon as we had finished, Alex removed the bowls and replenished our Killian's, and Jessie went to meet a challenge at the pool table. Alex and I waited for a dartboard and he trounced me badly two out of three, but somehow I managed to beat him once—though I think either he allowed it with intent or I got extremely lucky.

We drove home pleasantly satisfied with the evening and went shortly to bed. Sometimes just hanging out with friends is one of life's best pleasures, and this had been one.

Sometime in the middle of the night I woke in the dark, slipped out of bed, and went to the window, where I could see that snow was, as Alex had predicted, still falling, even more heavily than it had earlier.

Jessie will be delighted, I thought with a smile as I reached down to give Stretch a reassuring pat, for he had heard me rise and come to join me.

"Back to sleep, bitser," I told him, going back to bed myself. "It's not time to get up yet."

Satisfied, he lay down again on the rug and soon I could hear him snoring contentedly.

For me, sleep didn't come quite so fast or easily.

Thoughts of the woman I thought I had seen in the shop at Meta Rose Square kept me awake and wondering if it had been my imagination working overtime. But I didn't really think so. It was simply too much of a coincidence to have come out of nowhere to startle and worry me. Why in the world would she be following me around? And who was she?

For a few minutes I questioned it, found no answers, then gave myself a mental shake and decided to think about the upcoming holidays that were approaching rapidly and would require some early planning.

There should be at least one evening gathering of people we know and love, so I had to remember to ask Joe who he would like added to that invitation list. Rather than a sit-down dinner that would limit the number of friends we could invite, I decided that it should be a drop-in evening and would have food and drinks available for folks to help themselves.

Joe had told me that he and Sharon had already made their reservations with Alaska Airlines and Grant Aviation to arrive two days before Christmas and stay until just before New Year's for their trip back to Seattle. No, I remembered, they would be headed for Portland instead this time.

It would be fine to have them both for more than a weekend. I was pleased with Joe's choice of a future wife, knowing Sharon fit in easily and well, and was a kind and generous person who approached the world realistically and with a great sense of humor that suited my son—and me.

I wanted to ask her if she had any wishes or ideas for the gathering I was planning, as well as things she would like to see and do in Homer. Perhaps her family, like ours, had had holiday traditions she would like to add. I had to get a stocking made with her name on it to hang with Joe's on the mantel, for instance.

Besides Christmas, this visit would have wedding plans to be discussed and made. I would need to pursue the feasibility of having the ceremony on Niqa Island. How delightful, I thought, to anticipate a wedding for my son and his fine selection of spouse.

————————

I don't remember when I drifted off, but when I woke again it was just growing light outside, as usual in Alaska that time of year, when the window of daylight narrows considerably, doesn't show up till midmorning, and is gone again in midafternoon.

The splash of the shower running in the bathroom between my room and Alex and Jessie's told me it was time to get up. But, knowing that Stretch was probably more than ready to be taken outside for his morning constitutional, I put on my fleece robe and took him downstairs, where I slipped my bare feet into my boots and went out with him.

The snow had clearly continued to fall through the night and was still falling, so there was quite a bit on the ground. Each of the dog boxes in the yard had a five- or six-inch white addition crowning its roof and most of the dogs were content to stay dry and warmer inside those shelters.

A few, however, including Tank, were already up and out. Straining at the end of the tether that attached to his, he made it clear that he wanted to greet his small friend. Stretch, being much shorter legged, exhibited no desire to plow his way through the snow. So, while he piddled in the shelter of the stairs to the porch, I waded across to Tank and released him from the restraint that held him to his box.

As I followed him back, trying to walk in the prints I had made and failing, almost losing my balance once but somehow avoiding a fall into the deepening snow, the door opened and Jessie appeared on the porch.

"Good morning," she called from the top step. "Are you sure you've chosen the proper attire for playing in the snow this early?"

"I'm growing more certain by the moment that I haven't. But Stretch needed to go out and Tank wanted loose."

"Well, I was thinking that after breakfast I'd hitch up a team and take you for a ride on the sled, if you'd like that."

"I'd love it," I told her. "I've never been on a dog sled ride and I've lived here all my life. Can you imagine that?"

"Time to cure that situation, I think."

———————

So after breakfast we dressed warmly and I watched while Jessie hitched ten of her dogs to one of her smaller sleds, into which she had put two pillows for me to sit on. She tucked me in with a wool blanket and we were soon heading down the driveway toward the road. With Tank in the lead the dogs pulled enthusiastically, clearly excited to be back in harness and going somewhere.

At the end of the drive we turned right onto a trail that paralleled and was a bit below the road. The track had been broken earlier by snow machines and other dog sleds, so we went swiftly and smoothly along.

In about a mile Jessie turned the team onto a trail that gradually rose up a hill to the ridgeline, where we soon met another that she told me had been made by local mushers and was used for training away from the automobile traffic below.

It was lovely to be gliding along with snow-covered spruce mixed among the bare white trunks of birch on either side, the only sounds being the susurrus of the sled runners and the soft footfalls of the dogs on the snowy trail to break the silence of the winter woods.

"Oh, Jessie, thank you. This is wonderful," I told her over my shoulder to where she was riding the runners at the back of the sled. "No wonder you love it so much."

"Well," she said, "it's not always so nice, but days like this with lots of new snow sure do make it worthwhile. You should be along sometime when I take the mutts out on a trail through country that's really empty.

"Once, between here and Denali Park, we were traveling alone on a trail miles from any road. It was late and should have been dark, but the sky was bright with stars shining through an aurora display that spread green and red curtains across it like a net to hold their twinkling lights, and the light was reflected off the snow. That was one of the best ever! Sometimes you get lucky."

We soon came to a trail that led downhill and in minutes were coming back into Jessie's yard past the kennel sheds and the house. She called the dogs to a halt in the spot from which we had started, accompanied by the welcoming barks and howls from those that had been left behind in the yard and were clearly anxious for a turn of their own.

"They really do love to run, don't they," I said, climbing out of the sled reluctantly.

Jessie grinned and nodded. "As much as I do," she said. "Go ahead inside and warm up. I'm going to switch a couple of these guys and make another, longer run, but Alex will keep you provided with entertainment, I'm sure."

By the time I reached the door she had quickly traded two of the dogs in harness for others and was already in motion toward the road. Watching her over my shoulder, my hand on the doorknob, I was startled when Alex opened the door.

"Come on in," he invited, swinging it wide. "She's in her element and off for a couple of hours' run, I would guess. There's a fresh pot of coffee ready."

I removed my boots, coat, hat, and mittens, gave Stretch, who had come to greet me, a pat, and took Alex up on the coffee offer.

"I called again about those fingerprints," he told me, when we were seated at the table. "They've found absolutely no match in the system anywhere. Sorry."

"Well, it was worth a try. But isn't it a bit unusual in this day and age not to have your fingerprints somewhere?"

"Yes, but not unheard of. He's evidently never been arrested, applied for a government job, any other that required prints, or any one of a number of reasons he would have had them taken and, therefore, on file."

"A dead end, then," I said thoughtfully, and looked up to see a grin on his face as he shook his head. "No pun intended, I assure you."

"The world, and particularly the United States, has changed radically since nine-eleven," he said seriously. "We're so security-conscious that sometimes it makes me tired, even knowing most of it's necessary. Certainly makes my job more complicated at times. It's almost essential to have identification of some official kind— driver's license, passport, birth certificate . . . something."

"I can imagine. I just keep wondering why and how he would

come all the way to Alaska to commit suicide, and make sure that there was no way at all to establish his identity. Doesn't everybody leave a trail somewhere?"

"It clearly can be done with minute attention to details," Alex said, frowning. "I spoke to Alan Nelson in Anchor Point and they found nothing that would identify him as anything but the obviously false name he took."

"Why?" I said finally in frustration. "What could make anyone want to die anonymously, far from where he came from—wherever that was—and all alone?"

Alex simply shrugged and shook his head sadly at the idea.

"It must have made sense to him, I guess. But I can't fathom it."

Neither could I.

THIRTEEN

JESSIE CAME BACK A COUPLE OF HOURS LATER, traded most of her team for other dogs, took a sandwich and a thermos of hot coffee, and headed out again for another run. Late that afternoon she returned with a spring in her step and roses in her cheeks from the cold, a smile of satisfaction on her face as she came through the door after taking care of her dogs.

"What a great day," she said, shedding elbow-length mitts, parka, and boots by the door and coming sock-footed across the room. "I went all the way out to the airstrip at the end of Knik Road. Ran into half the racing community there or on the way. Everyone's taking advantage of the new snow."

Sinking into a chair at the table, she reached across for the Jameson bottle Alex had brought from the kitchen along with three glasses. She poured for each of us and raised hers in a toast. "Here's to winter showing up . . . finally. Now, what's making that great food smell coming from the kitchen? I'm starved."

"Onions, potatoes, and carrots, along with a small beef roast I dug out of the freezer this morning," Alex told her with a grin. "I had a hunch you'd be pleased to have dinner almost ready."

"You are a rare treasure of a man," she told him. "I think I'll keep you around a bit, if that suits you."

"Better wait and see how the food turns out," he teased.

We had a good dinner followed by a very casual, relaxed evening full of conversation and background music.

I took Stretch upstairs and went to bed just before eleven, knowing I should be up early for the next morning's drive to the Anchorage airport in order to catch my flight. It would get me to Homer at just after one o'clock to pick up the car I had left at the airport and make a quick stop for a few things at the grocery store on the way home.

Alex and Jessie weren't far behind me in retiring, for I heard them come up as I was drifting off and was thinking that running away from home had been a good thing to do, and that this place and these friends were just what I had needed.

We were all up fairly early that Sunday morning.

I packed up and brought my small bag downstairs and set it by the front door, ready to take to the car. My reservation with Grant Aviation was for just after noon, so I knew I had to leave Jessie's by nine to have plenty of time at the airport in Anchorage to return the rental car and check in for the flight. Luckily the items I had picked up on my shopping spree, along with the books I had been unable to resist, all fit easily into the bag and I would have little to carry once there.

We had a quick breakfast, said our good-byes with hugs and promises to get together again soon, and I was on my way as planned, waving out the car window to Jessie, Alex, and Tank, who were still standing on the front porch of the house to see me off.

It had evidently snowed in Eagle River and Anchorage as well, but the plows had been out on the Glenn Highway, so the drive was easier than I had expected. Without his ride-along basket from which to watch the world go by out the window, Stretch lay on the seat and took a nap for most of the trip, but periodically stood up on his hind legs to look out and check the passing scenery.

In just over an hour we had driven through Anchorage and arrived at the airport with plenty of time to spare. I turned in the rental car, took my baggage in a handy cart, and, with Stretch on his leash, made my way to the terminal to check in for the short flight home.

It's interesting how your mind turns homeward at the end of a trip. While I waited for the time to board the small plane, I found myself thinking of what I would want or need to do when I arrived back in Homer. I retrieved a notepad from my purse and made a list of what I wanted to remember to pick up at the grocery on the way home and remembered that I should also stop at the post office to check for mail. Between items, I hoped my answering machine would not be as full of the voices of people with questions about John Walker as I was afraid might have been left while I was away. I made up my mind to either ignore the machine completely or simply check and erase them all without returning the calls unless it concerned something else.

One good thing that running away from home had done for me was to give me a better perspective on that situation. I hadn't let

Trooper Nelson know I was leaving, so I hoped there hadn't been anything more he needed to talk with me about. Probably I should give him a call, I decided, but made up my mind to let it wait until the next day.

As I sat awaiting the boarding call, Stretch at my feet, I found myself looking around carefully to see if the woman who had been on the flight to Anchorage was anywhere to be seen. She was not. Very possibly, I decided, it had been my imagination and she hadn't really been following me at all. That was certainly feasible, wasn't it? Putting thoughts of her firmly out of my mind, I considered instead just how nice it would be to be back in my own cozy house again and returned to the list I had been making.

In just a few minutes boarding was announced. I put Stretch in his carrier and walked across the tarmac to the plane, where I once again took a rear seat and settled in for the short flight.

The day was overcast, but we left most of the snow behind in crossing the Kenai Peninsula and I could see as we landed that there was very little in Homer, and what there was wouldn't last long. Since our weather is almost always warmer than Anchorage's, it didn't surprise me, but I was glad that I wouldn't have to scrape a lot of ice and snow from my car before driving it home. Patient as only a machine can be, it had waited for me where I had left it in the parking lot in front of the terminal in a sunny spot, so it was bare of snow.

With my luggage in the backseat and Stretch happily ensconced once again in his basket, I pulled out and headed for the grocery as planned, then aimed the car for home, back in my town and pleased to be so, ready for some quality time in my own place.

What I anticipated and what I got turned out to be completely different things!

I pulled into my driveway, parked, and lifted Stretch down so he could go off to take care of business while I pocketed the keys and retrieved my baggage from the backseat of the car. By the time I approached the door, he was waiting, having scampered up the steps. Before I could reach out with the keys I had pulled from my coat pocket, he nosed at the door and without further assistance it swung open, allowing him inside and surprising me into frowning astonishment. I knew I had locked that door securely, as always, before I left.

Setting my bag down on the step, I cautiously pushed the door open wider and looked in. It was fairly dark inside, as I had, as usual upon leaving for any length of time, pulled closed the drapes that cover the sliding doors to the deck on the opposite side of the dining area after carefully locking them. But I noticed that one side was pulled askew, as if someone had moved it to look out. So, before investigating further, I reached to the wall beside the door and switched on both the kitchen and hallway lights.

What met my inspection was not what I had left at all.

After setting the grocery bag on the kitchen counter, I quickly went around turning on every electric light and pushed back the drapes. This let me see clearly that someone had spent time in my house.

While I am not the world's most meticulous housekeeper, I do like to have things in their places as much as possible, keep the floors clean on an as-needed basis, wipe the dust off surfaces that collect it, and wash all the windows spring and fall.

As I toured the kitchen, dining, and conversation areas I could

117

find nothing broken or removed, but a number of things had been noticeably moved from where I had left or kept them. The plant that lives on the dining table, for instance, was not in the middle as usual, but off center and closer to the far end. My canisters were no longer pushed back against the west wall on the kitchen counter under the cupboards, but were arranged neatly along the far end with their backs to the dining area. A large frying pan that I use so seldom I had almost forgotten I owned it and haven't taken out in months was propped in the dish drainer beside the sink. A book I had been reading and left on the sofa now occupied a corner of the fireplace hearth, not turned over with pages spread to keep my place, but closed neatly. The television set was not in its place, angled toward where I usually sat to watch it from the sofa, but had been rolled back a bit and turned toward a chair several feet away.

There were other things that caught my attention as I made a more careful inventory of the place. Nothing seemed to be missing or broken, just out of order—moved to fit another person's preferences.

Stretch, satisfied to be home, had gone across the room and was lying on the rug next to that hearth, as always, and was watching me move about the room with interest, having no idea that anything was wrong. I left him there and made a determined examination of the rest of the house, upstairs and down.

Someone had been in my house and evidently for some period of time. Whoever it was had stayed awhile—long enough to examine or use and move all the things I had noticed, but had left them undamaged and neat enough that they had expected no notice.

Maybe!

Or could this have been done with intent to concern the only person who would detect such insignificant details? *Me!* If that were the case—then the remaining question was *why?* And, of course, *who?*

Across from the fireplace seating area is the door that leads to a small room in the northeast corner of the downstairs that my Daniel and I had used as an office and that I still keep for that purpose. There I found less care and more intent in a search by whoever it had been. Papers that I had neatly sorted and placed in piles of things I needed to keep or attend to were now scattered across the desk, as if someone had been searching for something in particular. What? One deep drawer that held filing folders was open maybe half an inch, but nothing in it seemed out of place.

There are three phones in my house. One sits on the counter between the kitchen and dining areas, with the answering machine attached. Another is upstairs next to my bed, and the third is on the desk in the office. The red light on the answering machine had been blinking furiously when I passed it, but I had expected that and meant to ignore it for the time being.

I left the office, collected my traveling bag, and went upstairs. There I found more personal evidence of an intruder.

Two pillows on my bed were not in the positions in which I had left them, one on top of the other, but had been plumped up and placed separately at the head of the bed. The bedcovers that I had thrown back when I got up on the day I departed had been pulled up neatly with the top edge of the sheet smoothed down over the top edge of the blanket. I pulled the covers back to look at the sheets, and it was not my eyes but my nose that told me someone had slept in my bed, for a faint whiff of an unfamiliar perfume floated up in my face.

Though it was not a particularly unpleasant scent, it was one I did not recognize or could identify as worn by anyone I knew.

I sneezed.

With that sneeze I was suddenly not anxious but furious!

With angry hands I yanked the bed clean of sheets, blanket, pillowcases, and mattress pad. I gathered them all up, took them out of the room, and tossed them down to the foot of the stairs.

Before following them, I went into the bathroom across the hall. There I found more evidence of intrusion. My toothpaste was not in the small cabinet above the sink where I kept it, but lay on the edge of the sink beside a faucet.

Angrily I tossed it immediately into the wastebasket.

The shower curtain that I only pull across on its rod to keep water from splashing out had been left pulled across, not pushed back into folds at the head of the tub as I would automatically have done. A clean bath towel and washcloth that had not been in the bathroom when I left, but had evidently been rummaged from the linen closet in the hall, had been neatly hung from the shower curtain rod as well. They were now dry, as were the tub and the sink, so whoever had used them had been gone for at least a day—long enough for its dampness to evaporate.

They followed the bedcovers to the bottom of the stairs, along with all the other towels and washcloths that had been in the bathroom.

I followed them down.

After gathering up and separating the items, I stuffed half, the sheets, pillowcases, and all the bathroom towels and washcloths, into the washing machine in the hallway closet, poured in not just detergent but bleach as well, and started the machine, leaving the second load, blanket and mattress cover, to follow as soon as possible.

Stretch is no dummy. He picks up on my moods, but I am seldom angry. So, as I took care of tossing in the laundry with annoyance and just a hint of fear beginning to surface, he had detected that something was wrong and come trotting across the room. Without a sound he stood next to me, looking up with a quizzical cock of his head.

It broke my anger.

"Ah, lovie. What would I do without you?" I told him as I reached down to pick him up and carry him to one of the dining chairs, where I sat down, placed him on my lap, and gave him several reassuring pats.

He licked my hand, assuming that I was back to normal.

When he wanted down I lowered him to the floor, got up, and went into the kitchen. There I readied the pot with water and coffee, put away the few groceries I had brought home, then stood staring out the window at nothing in particular as the pot made its usual gurgles and sighs. When it finished working I took a cup of it back to the table. There, I sat looking out through the glass doors onto the deck, the bay, and the snow-covered mountains to the south, letting my mind review the situation, assessing what I had found and knew, and what I wanted to know, letting go of the resentment and suspicion for the moment.

Someone, without my permission or knowledge, had somehow entered and used my house—my private, familiar, and safe place—as if it were a hotel. She had felt free to cook in my kitchen, watch my television, relax in my living room, sort through my office, and, as I had discovered was the last straw, had slept in my very own bed.

When? I wondered.

While I had been gone, obviously.

But for how long?

Then I realized what I had said to myself in making assumptions.

She!

I had said *she*!

Aside from that hint of unfamiliar fragrance that had risen from the sheets on my bed as I pulled back the covers, there was nothing I could think of that had told me for certain it had been a woman. But somehow I simply knew that it had been. There wasn't a shadow of a doubt in my mind, but I had no way to prove it, had I?

None at all!

FOURTEEN

As I sat there at the table, feeling uncertain in my own home, far from easy in the well-known space, the phone rang, and without thinking I went to the counter and answered it.

"Maxie?"

"Yes."

"This is Andy at the bookstore. I've been trying to reach you for the last few days. You must have been out of town."

So that solved one or two of the blinks from the answering machine.

"I was in Wasilla, visiting friends," I told him. "Got back just this afternoon from Anchorage."

"Oh—well, glad you're back. Hope you had a good trip."

"I did, thank you."

"Well, I've got something I want to show you—something I found in one of those books you returned. Could you come over to the store?"

I hesitated for a moment, trying to decide if I wanted to leave just then, after finding that an unknown someone had been staying in my house. Thinking I might—probably should—call the police about it.

Andy waited for a few seconds, then said, "I think you'll want to see this. It's something Walker probably used as a bookmark, that he must have left in one of those books by mistake."

That quickly made up my mind.

It would not take long to drive across our small town and see what it was he had found. I could be back in about half an hour.

"Okay, I'll be there shortly," I told him.

After calling Stretch, who I had no intention of leaving at home alone, I put my coat and boots back on, took my purse under one arm, Stretch under the other, and went out, closing and locking the door securely behind me.

As I moved onto the driveway, heading for my car, I glanced to my right along the side of the house and stopped abruptly, frowning at a thing I hadn't noticed on arrival.

Along the side of the building, in its shadow, lay a light and now sublimating layer of snow that the winter sun, low in the south this time of year, could not reach to warm and melt. Imprinted in it clearly were the prints someone's boots had left. In a fairly straight line they continued to the northeast corner of the house and disappeared around it.

Without releasing Stretch, I followed, stepping carefully to one side so as not to disturb the prints to and around the corner, then continued along the east side of the house. Where enough sun had reached to melt the snow from the frozen grass of my lawn, they had disappeared, but clearly someone—probably the same someone I had found evidence of inside—had walked around, probably to see if they could gain entry from the opposite side.

I returned to the front driveway, put Stretch into his basket, went around the car, and was about to climb in myself when a thought stopped me.

How had this woman opened my back door? It had been not just unlocked, but slightly open when we arrived home—evidence of her leaving in a hurry perhaps. But how had it been opened?

I went back to take a closer look at the door and found no scratches around the lock or breakage of the frame that would be evidence of force used to gain entry. So she must have been very clever at picking locks, or . . .

I had taken the house key with me on the ring with my car key and a couple of others that were less often used. One of them was for a lock on a shed on the west side of the drive, though it was seldom used unless I was going to be gone for a long time and hadn't been secured before I left for Anchorage. This building had been intended as a garage, but through the years it had filled up with extraneous tools and gardening equipment that eventually came to have their home there: bags of grass seed and fertilizer, the lawn mower, hoses and sprinklers, shovels, rakes, hoes, flowerpots, screwdrivers, hammers, saws, and so forth.

I looked in that direction, reminded that inside the door to the shed I had pounded a nail into the wall to hold an extra house key, should I ever lose my keys or find myself locked out for some other reason. I went quickly across the drive, opened the door, and found that nail . . . *empty*!

That solved the mystery of her uninvited entry. Whoever it was who had used my house as a place to stay had looked for and found the extra key and used it, obviously. But where was that key now? Clearly, as Stretch had been able to push the house door open when we arrived, she hadn't used it to lock the door when she left and I hadn't found it anywhere inside.

Should I have the house door lock changed? It seemed advisable. But it was Sunday and there would probably be no one to call until the following day. So I decided that I would find someone to do the job the next morning and, in the meantime, should go to and come back from Andy's as quickly as possible, shouldn't I?

I closed the shed door, got into the car, and headed for the bookstore.

Andy was talking to a customer when I arrived. One I was glad to see—Lew Joiner.

They both greeted me with smiles.

"I'm glad you're here, Lew," I told him. "I picked up a couple of books for you at Annabel's in Wasilla—ones I don't think you have on the Revolution. Why don't you stop by on your way home for them?"

"So you've been up to the big city and beyond," he said with a smile. "I'd be glad to stop, but I want to go upstairs and peruse Andy's history section first. Will you be home by then?"

"Yes, definitely. I'll leave the door unlocked, so just come on in."

Lew headed upstairs and we heard his footsteps overhead as he went directly to the history books he loved.

I turned to Andy, who had picked up one of the books I had taken to him on Monday, almost a week ago. He laid it on the counter and I could see that he had put a marker about halfway through it.

"I was flipping through this, like I always do to make sure books are in good shape before I shelve them. About halfway through it, between the pages I found this."

He opened the book and I saw that the marker was a color photograph the size of a three-by-five filing card.

"Here," he said, holding it out to me. "See what you think, if anything."

The picture showed the head and shoulders of an attractive woman with dark hair and brown eyes who was wearing a blue sweater over a white blouse with the top two buttons open, a silver hoop earring. She was looking back over her right shoulder at whoever held the camera with a pleasant, if slightly surprised, smile. There were trees in the background and a bit of grass. Between and beyond the trees were a couple of tall buildings.

There was nothing to identify the location, but there was something vaguely familiar about it. The feeling faded as I stared at her.

"Turn it over," Andy instructed.

I did as directed, and as I flipped it the hint of a familiar scent wafted up to tickle my nose—lavender. Someone must have sprayed perfume on the back's more absorbent paper, for there was a slight stain near one lower corner and the scent was strongest there.

There were words on that side as well, in small and neat handwriting:

> *Smells are surer than sounds or sights*
> *to make the heartstrings crack.*
> KIPLING

That was all. There was no name to identify the subject, no date, no indication as to where the picture had been taken, who had taken it, or who it had belonged to. But since the book had been John Walker's, I thought that either it had been his or he had found it and left it in the book. Somehow I doubted the latter.

I couldn't help feeling that it *had* been his. That not only had he carried it with him from wherever he had come from, but that this woman had been important enough in his life to make him keep it as one of the few things he carried, and carefully, where he could look at it often. She had meant something special to him, as had the scent of lavender he had associated with her.

"Well?" Andy questioned. "What do you think?"

"I think I should give it to Trooper Nelson," I told him. "Though I doubt it will do him much good. And that was all, right? There wasn't anything in the other book, was there?"

"No." He shook his head. "I went through both of them twice, but there was nothing but that."

"And you're sure this wasn't left by some previous reader?"

"Very sure. I flip through all of them before I put them on the shelves. Sometimes people leave odd things that they've used for bookmarks. Last winter I found Jake Leary's daughter's birth certificate in one he brought in. These days a lot of people use Post-it notes, but mostly I find that whoever buys a book uses the purchase receipt. It's already tucked into the book, so it makes a convenient marker."

I put the photograph in my purse and took it with me.

When I returned to the car, I found Stretch snoozing in his basket, but he woke immediately, glad to see me and, as always, eager to be off.

"You are a wonky bitser, you are," I told him, using one of my Daniel's Aussie expressions. He stood up in the basket, ready to see whatever there was to see. He never tires of traveling around with me. Nor do I with him, for that matter.

On the way home I swung by Ulmer's to pick up a new lock for my door, having decided that with the key missing from the shed I would be wise to replace it as soon as possible. Besides, Lew would soon show up, and maybe I would ask him to do the replacing in exchange for the books I had brought him from Annabel's.

I found a new lock with a couple of new and different keys. It seemed pretty much like the old one, and so would require little or no refitting in terms of the door. I knew that I could have done it myself, but Lew would do it better and likes helping sometimes. It makes him feel useful to be asked.

Shortly after I reached home and had established that no one had made use of my house in the hour I was gone, Lew showed up and cheerfully agreed to replace the lock, which he did in just a few minutes, using my tools.

"There you go," he said when finished. "All secure. But there really didn't seem to be a thing wrong with the old one."

"I know and there wasn't. But there's a lost key floating around somewhere and I'll feel better knowing I have complete control of the lock and won't have to consider hitting some burglar with a cast-iron skillet."

He laughed at that image, agreeing that whatever made me feel better was worth it, and we sat down for the coffee I had poured while he worked and the books I had brought from Annabel's.

I saw no reason to tell him about the unwelcome visitor who had used my house while I was away. Lew, like a lot of men I know, tends to be protective of women, and knowing about it would make him uneasy, even now that he had rectified the problem with the new lock.

At least I certainly hoped he had and felt better knowing the job was done.

So we discussed books, as we often did, and after a second cup of coffee, he said he was off to home.

He thanked me for the books. I thanked him for the lock installation. Then I waved him off from the door and he returned the wave out the window of his yellow pickup.

How nice it is to have good friends with similar interests.

FIFTEEN

HAVING THE DOOR OPEN AS LEW WORKED had cooled off the house considerably, but it was worth it for the relief at having the old lock now solidly replaced. I had pulled the drapes back across the sliding door to the deck before I left, but it was already growing dark outside as usual this late in the year, so I left them drawn. I turned up the thermostat to start the furnace and carried a few small logs across the room to the fireplace, where I started a small blaze to help take off the chill of the room.

Having a fire burning lifts the mood of a room considerably whether you really need its heat or not, though it takes a few minutes to warm up the space around it even with the furnace working. While I waited, I gave Stretch a bit of kibble and made myself a peanut butter and jelly sandwich to accompany a mug of tomato soup—comfort food. As I sat down at the table to eat, on the table beside me I laid the *Homer News*, a half-size local paper that comes out once a week on Wednesday and had arrived while I was away.

On the front page below the fold was a short article on the demise of John Walker. I don't know why it should have surprised me. Homer is a small town and anything the least bit interesting or exciting always makes the front page. I should have anticipated that, as usual, some reporter would have the duty of checking the law enforcement reports for both the troopers and the local police for the past week, and a suicide would definitely catch attention.

The article was short and carried only the direct facts of how he supposedly died and how he was found. My name was not mentioned, thanks be. As the person who had found him, Julia Bennet at the Driftwood Inn was, of course. But others not mentioned had met him, including those who had gathered at my house for dinner the weekend before and Andy at the bookstore. I imagined that there must be a few more. He had mentioned a planned trip to the museum and had told me that first day that he would go across the street to Duggan's pub, where many local people gathered to enjoy company, food, drink, and games of darts and pool.

After finishing my soup and sandwich, I rinsed out the bowl, carried the paper across the room, and sat down near the fire, which was now burning cheerfully. I turned on a lamp next to my chair and thumbed through the rest of the paper, but there was nothing else that caught my attention, so I laid it down and thought about the whole thing a bit.

Remembering the picture Andy had found in one of the O'Brian books, I got up and went to find it in my purse. I sat down again and took the time to examine it more closely.

The woman in the photo did not resemble Walker in the slightest. Her face was thinner than his and her hair and eyes dark. It was impossible to tell how tall she was, or how much she might have weighed, but I felt she was slim, for her collarbone, a bit of which showed in the open neckline of her blouse, was well defined and the shoulder that was turned toward the camera did not look heavy.

Several things about the picture suggested to me that this woman had been well known to John.

The first was that he had taken the picture at all, and I was somehow sure that he had held the camera. Seldom does anyone take that kind of photograph of someone they do not know and want to record—a professional photographer, perhaps, but not a stranger in what appeared to be a park on a sunny afternoon.

I knew I was making assumptions, but at least a couple of them must be at least close to correct, so I continued.

The second thing about the picture was the woman's expression in looking back at him as she half turned away. She was smiling and the hint of surprise in that smile—both in her eyes and on her mouth—held a sense of what almost was and might have become laughter at his impulsive action with the camera. It implied a tolerance as well, and I couldn't help thinking that this was not the first time he had taken her picture on impulse and that he had wanted to do so for his own reasons. There was confidence and caring in the taking of it and caring that was returned in her allowance, even indulgence, of it.

The picture I held was not new. The edges showed some wear and it was curled a little, as if it might have been carried in a wallet. It might have been a thing out of Walker's past—a relationship that didn't last maybe, but that he had valued enough to keep the photo as a reminder—a memory.

But if it was so dear to him, why would he have left it as a marker in a book he read and wanted returned to Andy's?

I turned it over to read the line by Kipling that someone, probably Walker, had written on the back: *Smells are surer than sounds or sights to make the heartstrings crack.* And once again that faint whiff of lavender rose from the reverse of the picture, somehow tying together the woman and the scent. Both must have had meaning to him.

Then I turned it back and looked carefully at what I could see of the setting beyond the woman in the photo. There was nothing specific to identify the location, but as before, there was something vaguely familiar about it. It was not a place I knew or could recall, but could have been anywhere in a city with tall buildings near a park, for it seemed like a park with lawns, and the trees from their size had been there for many years, were not newly planted. So it was some well-established city, but could be almost anywhere in the Lower Forty-eight. Our trees in Alaska are mainly birch and spruce and those in the photograph looked more like oak, or maple, or—some other deciduous variety with heavy trunks and broader leaves.

As I considered it there was a sudden knock at the door. Still cautious, I went and peered out the window before answering.

It was Lew again.

"Hey," he said, stepping in as I opened, then closed the door against the outside chill. "I forgot I wasn't using my own tools and took your screwdriver along home with me. Didn't notice till I started to put it in my toolbox and thought I'd better return it before it got mixed with mine and you—thinking I'd heisted it—would never share books with me again. Sorry."

He handed me the offending article with a grin.

"As if that's likely to happen," I told him. "But thanks for bringing it back. If you knew how seldom I use it, you'd know I'd never have figured out where it went and just assume I'd done the losing."

"How about I make it up to you," he suggested with another grin. "I'm headed down to Duggan's to grab a bite and a beer. Why don't you come along? My treat."

It sounded like a good idea to me, but as I started to agree I remembered why I had wanted that lock replaced.

"Thanks, Lew," I told him, turning from where I had been reaching for the coat I had left on one of the hooks near the door. "There was a problem while I was gone and I think I'd better stick around home for a few days."

He cocked his head questioningly. "What kind of problem? Something I can fix?"

"No. But . . ."

"What?"

"Well . . . Oh, what the hell! Someone without an invitation got in and stayed in my house while I was gone and I want to be here if she comes back."

He frowned in concern.

"You mean someone that you don't know just broke in?"

"Yes. Stayed for a couple of nights, I'd guess. Whoever it was had gone when I came back today, but she didn't break in."

"How'd she get in? Your lock was okay."

"I think that's where the extra key in the shed went—the one that's not there now. I'm assuming she took it and, since she didn't put it back, might show up again."

"Good thing I changed that lock. Who do you think it was?"

"I've no idea. But it wasn't anyone we know. Our friends and acquaintances would have asked first, or at the very least left me a note."

"Or found themselves a hotel room," he suggested. "Sounds to me like some stranger who didn't want anyone to know where they were in town. How did this person know you were out of town and your house was empty?"

"I don't know. But she was confident enough of it to stay a night, maybe two."

"And how do you know it was a she? Could have been a he."

"I don't think so. From the traces I found moved and used I think it was a woman. Would an itinerant man have carefully made the bed in the morning and put things away in the kitchen?"

He grinned. "Okay, you're probably right. I almost never make mine, but that's only since I lost Hilda. She'd never have left ours unmade."

Lew's wife had passed ten or twelve years before, which—I had always thought—was a large part of the reason he tended to bury himself in books.

"Have you told the police?" he asked with a concerned frown.

"No. Aside from the fact that someone was here, what could I tell them? I didn't see her and she didn't leave anything personal that I can find."

"Still, I think you should," he said. "Think about it anyway. They might find fingerprints at least. You call if you need me, okay?"

I agreed and he started to turn toward the door, hesitated, then swung back to me.

"You know," he said thoughtfully. "Last Friday evening at Duggan's there was a strange woman. . . . By *strange* I don't mean weird, just not local. But there was this woman and she was asking about you."

I was instantly focused and interested.

"What was she asking?"

"Well, it *was* Friday and the place was pretty full of customers and noise after work. She was a couple of seats away from me at the bar, so I couldn't hear the conversation she was having with Bill Jessup, but I heard your name mentioned and could tell she was asking questions. That's about it."

"What did she look like?"

Lew thought for a moment, then said slowly, "Can't tell you how tall she was because she was sitting down, but she was younger than us, in her thirties, probably pushing forty, I'd guess. She was wearing a green jacket that probably matched her slacks—looked like a suit jacket. You know—an outfit. Under it she had on a shirt with small green stripes and a white collar. Her hair was dark and straight—cut about chin level, a little longer in the front."

"Any jewelry?"

"Didn't notice any, but I wasn't paying much attention, you understand. Only looked that direction when I heard your name mentioned, so that's about all I know."

I nodded, thinking that his description didn't sound like the woman on the plane to Anchorage that I had also seen in the hotel and thought I had seen in the Wasilla cooking store. It didn't sound like the woman in John Walker's picture, either. But I knew I was only thinking of her because of the photograph.

"Listen, Maxie," Lew said, giving me a concerned look. "Would you like me to stay, just in case this intruder comes back? You've got an extra bedroom and I'd be glad to."

I had to smile at the thought, however generously it was offered.

"You want to start gossip spreading through the whole town?" I teased him. "I appreciate the offer, Lew. Really. But I have a new lock now, thanks to you. I promise that I'll tell the police about my intruder and, for tonight, I'll keep the shotgun where I can reach it, along with my cell phone. Stretch is as good as an alarm anyway. Should anyone try to get in, he'd let me know immediately. I'll be fine, but thanks for the offer."

"Well—anything happens, you call me, right? I can be here in just a few minutes."

"Okay. I will, I promise."

SIXTEEN

It was a quiet evening.

I had checked the messages left on the answering machine and found two from Andy, but no others that required my immediate attention, so I ignored them for the time being and settled myself to watch *60 Minutes* on television.

It felt good to be back in my own house, though I had enjoyed doing a little shopping in Anchorage and visiting with Alex and Jessie.

I thought I heard a car in my drive, but when I went to look out the kitchen window I could see that it was just the neighbor who lived directly across the street pulling into his. There is a sensor over my door that automatically turns on a light to illuminate my drive and that side of the house when anything or anyone comes close enough to activate it. That light was not on, but I could see far enough into what was now total darkness outside to see that it was once again snowing lightly. Thin, feathery white flakes were falling through the still, dark air to already have touched the drive, the shed, and the part of the yard that I could see with a thin coat of white. It was very quiet in that silence that gently falling snow seems to bring.

It might have been dark and cold outside, but it was warm and cozy inside. So, for the time being, I gave up speculations on who had been in my house while I was away and whether it might have been the woman Lew had mentioned seeing at Duggan's bar. Instead, when *60 Minutes* was over I turned off the television, propped the shotgun within reach as I had promised Lew, and settled myself comfortably on the sofa to start one of the Ellis Peters mysteries I had picked up at Annabel's.

Stretch had already gone out and come quickly back inside, shaking a scanty amount of snow from his feet that instantly melted into several small puddles, which I had wiped up with a paper towel. He had then settled in his usual place on the rug in front of the fireplace and was snoozing. Mixed with the crackle of the firewood burning I could hear his small snore from where I sat on the sofa and had to smile. He is such good company, interested in almost everything, well behaved, and never boring.

Thank you, Daniel, I thought, not for the first time. What would I do without Stretch's company?

When my Daniel died, Stretch had wandered around for days expecting his lord and master to come home, but slowly seemed to accept that I was all he had left and decided that he would have to be responsible for me instead. He still thinks he is, and perhaps, in a way, he's right.

I was totally relaxed, warm from the fire and the afghan I had tossed over my legs, and well into the third chapter of the story when I fell asleep with the book in my lap.

I was startled awake and sitting straight up, ready for fight or flight, at the sound of someone knocking on my door.

Stretch was on his feet and barking as he headed toward the door to guard his territory—and mine.

The insistent knocking stopped for a moment as someone rang the doorbell. Then it started again. It sounded important—or demanding. I couldn't decide which, but really didn't care as I picked up the shotgun, tucked it under my arm with the barrel pointed at the floor, and headed for the door, sending Stretch back into the living room as I passed him.

"Stay and hush!" I told him, so he did both, but made it clear with a small growl that it was not his choice.

Retreating a foot or two, he stopped barking, but remained a few steps behind me intending defense, should he decide it was necessary and shouldn't be left to me. It always amuses me that such a small being, so low to the ground and short-legged, should be so fearless and determined to protect his place and people.

Instead of going directly to the door, I went to the kitchen window, from which I could see most of the yard and front step.

There was a car next to mine in the drive and someone's footprints in the snow led from it to where she stood on that step, right hand raised to knock again, but in the darkness I couldn't see who it was.

I reached for the switch between the window and the door and turned the outside light on.

The expected knock did not happen. Evidently the woman had decided that her summons was about to be answered. She waited, looking down, and I couldn't see her face, but could tell she was not someone I recognized as having seen before.

After laying the shotgun on the kitchen counter within easy reach, I went around to the door, opened it to the length of the chain that keeps it from opening completely, and peered out at the woman who stood there, now looking up.

She was, as expected, completely unknown to me.

For some reason I had expected that it might be the woman who had flown with me to Anchorage, who I had definitely seen in the Hilton Hotel, and possibly caught a glimpse of in Wasilla. This was a different, thinner face. Her dark hair was shorter, and she wore glasses. It was also not the woman in the photograph that Andy had found in the O'Brian book I had returned for John Walker. But there was something about her . . .

"Can I help you?" I asked.

She looked at me silently for a moment, then nodded.

"I think maybe you can," she said. "Please, could I come in and talk with you?"

"What about?" I asked.

She looked down again, hesitated for a moment, then squared her shoulders, looked up, and took a deep breath.

"I think you knew my brother—John," she said in a voice that hoped I would believe her.

———

I was so astonished that for a moment or two I couldn't say anything or move. I stood staring at her as the idea took hold.

It was her eyes that convinced me. They had a tired, haunted look that made me feel that I should accept what she said. I could believe that she *was* his sister—a little younger, not so tall, but somehow I thought she was telling me the truth, though she didn't look like him.

"Let me open the door," I told her, then closed it enough to slip the chain out of its track and opened it wide so she could step in. I closed it behind her and invited her to hang the coat she was wearing on one of the handy hooks.

She nodded, took it off, and tucked her gloves into one of the pockets before turning to me.

"Thank you," she said, with a wide-eyed glance at the shotgun on the counter.

"Don't let that worry you," I assured her. "I just came back from a trip and found that someone had been staying uninvited in my house while I was gone. I'm just a bit flinchy at the moment . . . probably being excessively cautious."

"It wasn't me," she assured me quickly.

"I'm glad to hear that. I live alone, except for Stretch, the bonzer boy here," I said and waved a hand at him. He had come closer, seeing from my actions that this person was acceptable and expecting to be introduced.

"Hello, Stretch," she told him, crouching to give him a pat. "I like your name."

He licked her hand in acceptance as she smiled and rubbed his ears.

Hardly anyone can resist those liquid coffee eyes.

Rising, she turned back to me and held out a hand.

"I haven't introduced myself," she said. "I'm Amy Fletcher, John's sister. And I already know that you're Mrs. McNabb."

"Just Maxie, please," I responded. "Everyone calls me Maxie. It's good to meet you, Amy. Come and sit down and I'll make us both a cup of tea."

She sat at the dining table and watched as I put the kettle on to heat water for the tea before joining her across its width.

"However did you find me?" I asked her.

"The woman at the Driftwood Inn gave me your name last Friday and a nice man at the bar across the street told me where you lived. I came by that day and Saturday, but you weren't here."

"And John? How did you know it was your brother? He seems to have taken great care that no one would know who he really was, where he came from, or why. How did you know he had been staying at the Driftwood?"

She sighed and a sad and tired kind of resignation narrowed her eyes.

"I saw the article in the paper," she said, "and knew it was my brother. There were a couple of reasons for my knowing.

"First, I knew that he had always wanted to come to Alaska. He used to talk about it frequently and I remember knowing things about glaciers and polar bears and mountains, because John told me and showed me pictures. He had a collection of books and videos about Alaska. When I lost track of him in Seattle, I decided he might have gone north, so I gave it a try.

"Second, after all my searching I knew he wasn't using his real name—didn't want to be found. He had walked away from everything and everyone in his life when his wife died. I think he just couldn't stay in the city and be confronted every day with the fact that she was gone. I can understand that. They really loved each other, were like two halves of the same person in a way. I don't think that happens very often and he simply didn't know how and didn't want to live there without her.

"It took me a long while, years, to look for him state by state, city after city, clue by clue. But then I showed his picture to a trucker in New Mexico and learned that he was using an assumed name. I knew he had in other places he passed through and that sometimes they were, like John Walker, taken straight off whiskey bottles. Jack Daniel was one, Austin Nichols, another—that one when he was working construction in Texas. He must have found a way to forge the identification that he needed.

"I never caught up with him—just found clues to where he had been when I got there too late. But after I became convinced that he wasn't dead and had just walked away, I knew I had to try, so I started hunting every time I could take off from my job. Two years ago I gave that up and started looking almost full-time, taking a part-time job, whatever I could find when I ran low on money. I only found where he had been temporarily—jobs he had worked for a short period of time. You see, he never stayed anywhere long enough for me to catch up with him. So I tracked him through trial and error from one place to another. My finding my way here is just the end of a very long road for me—eight years of off-and-on searching in a lot of places. You see, for a time I was in shock—so sure he was dead. By the time I started looking he was long gone and difficult to follow."

. . . the end of a very long road . . . I caught the phrase and remembered once again what John had said the day I met him: *Maybe I'll decide to spend what's left of my life at the end of the road.* So he had. And now, she had come there as well—unfortunately too late.

"Do you have a picture of your brother?" I asked, convinced, but wanting to make sure we were really talking about the same person.

"Yes." She had brought a shoulder bag to the table with her and now reached into it for a notebook with many fat pages that seemed filled with writing. From between those pages she took a photograph and handed it across to me.

It was not a snapshot, but a professional photograph. But it *was* John—the man I had first met out on the spit—looking straight into the camera. He was dressed much differently, however, in a dark gray suit, white shirt, and red tie with tiny blue stripes, neat and professional looking. His hair was shorter than it had been as I knew him, but his smile was the same, warm, self-confident, and friendly. He looked quite a bit younger than the man I had met, and certainly less worn. I remembered the lines in his forehead and around his mouth and eyes that were not evident in the picture. His shoulders had been broader and I remembered his scarred and callused hands.

I nodded and handed it back.

"This is a younger John than I met. Did you take the picture?" I asked Amy.

"No. I found it in their apartment after . . . well, later. Probably taken by some office photographer. But I think his wife, Marty, may have taken it. Not long after they were married in nineteen ninety-eight."

"He was married?"

"Yes. And I thought for some time that they had both died at work when the World Trade Center towers fell. They both worked there, you see. That's where they met.

"Marty died. They never found her body, like many others. But

146

things I found out made me believe that John had not been killed too. Days later, a coworker of his who made it out told me that he was sure John was gone on some business errand that morning and wasn't in his office in the second tower. But another survivor said that he had come back just before the first plane hit. It was confusing, but enough to make me believe he might be alive and to start me hunting.

"I went to their apartment. At first I couldn't bear to go there, but less than a week after the attack on the towers I did and I found some things missing that should have been there if he was dead—small things I figured that he had probably taken with him: their wedding picture, for instance, some casual clothing he wouldn't have worn to the office—jeans, a sweatshirt or two, a heavy jacket, underwear, socks. His shaving gear was missing."

"Stay here a minute," I said, getting up. "There's something I want to show you."

I crossed the room, took the photograph Andy had found in the book, and returned to her side of the table. Holding it out to her, I told her, "This was in a book he was reading and left for me. Is this his wife—Marty? I assume from the background it was taken in New York—Central Park, yes?"

She stared at it as if she was looking at a ghost and there were tears in her eyes when she looked up and nodded.

"Yes. And John took the picture. That's easy to tell from her expression. He often took snapshots of her—had several in his office and at home."

Then she burst into a flood of tears.

SEVENTEEN

THE TEARS LASTED ONLY THE AMOUNT OF TIME it took me to hand Amy the box of tissues I keep on the kitchen counter.

I had a feeling that she had cried herself pretty much dry of them years before and that they were at least partially inspired by the relief she was feeling in at least having answers *at the end of the road* she had followed for such a long time.

How many people would undertake such a far-reaching and dedicated search for someone they loved?

It made me sad that she couldn't have arrived just a few days earlier.

"Have you talked with the police or the troopers? There is a trooper who was called to the scene at the Driftwood Inn."

"No, but I should, I suppose. It really doesn't matter now, does it? The woman at the Driftwood told me they had taken John's body to Anchorage to try to find out who he was."

I was a little surprised that she had not contacted law enforcement.

"Yes, you should," I told her. "I know Trooper Nelson and can call him if you want. He can tell you much more than I can. It's a little late now, but tomorrow morning will do, yes?"

She nodded.

"Why don't you stay here tonight?" I asked.

"Oh, I couldn't put you out—" she began.

I interrupted. "You won't. I have an extra bedroom across the hall from mine upstairs and would be pleased to have you. We can make that call to Trooper Nelson in the morning and I can introduce you."

"Are you sure?"

"Yes, definitely. It would make things easier for you, I think, that I've already talked to him. He's really very nice. You can tell him what you've told me and answer most of the questions he's been finding dead ends to."

She agreed and went to the car to bring in a small suitcase while I called Julia Bennet at the Driftwood to let her know that Amy would be staying with me and wouldn't need a room.

I took her upstairs and showed her to the one across the hall from mine that has always belonged to son Joe, where he and Sharon slept when they came from Seattle and would again at Christmas. When he left I had washed the sheets and pillowcases and remade the bed, so I knew it was clean and ready for a new occupant. I also gave her clean towels and showed her the upstairs bathroom.

She thanked me profusely and, though it was late, came back down for a last cup of tea, at my suggestion.

"Sleepytime Tea," she said with a smile, reading the box the herb tea had come in, while I poured hot water onto the tea bags in our mugs. "Appropriate."

"No caffeine, you'll notice," I told her as I handed her a mug of it. "Sugar?"

She took a sip. "No, thanks. This is fine as it is."

We moved to the sofa near the now dying fire, where Stretch had already gone to lie down on his rug. I took my usual place at one end. Amy sat down at the other with a sigh of relaxation.

"You have such a sweet, cozy house," she said. "You must love living here."

I told her that my first husband, Joe senior, the fisherman, had built the house somewhat in the style of cottages in the fishing villages of New England, with similar two stories and a widow's walk up top.

"You must have lived here a long time."

"All my life, bred and born here. Not in this house, of course. Grew up, went to school here, college in Seattle, married twice—good men, both gone now. The first, Joe, left me this house, and, besides financial independence, the second, my Aussie husband, Daniel, left me Stretch, who was his dog when we met."

At the sound of his name Stretch raised his head, gave me a look, knowing he was, as he often is, a topic of conversation, then laid it down again after a yawn.

He's getting older now—will be nine on his next birthday in March. Dachshunds have a life expectancy of twelve to fourteen years typically, so though he's healthy and I don't expect him to kick the bucket anytime soon, I do conscientiously make sure that he sees the vet on a regular basis and gets enough exercise and proper food. I know I'm going to miss him dearly when he's gone to join Daniel.

"I haven't been here in the winter for several years," I told Amy.

"I have a motor home that I've taken to the Southwest in the fall, then driven back up the Alaska Highway in the spring. I've had the best of both worlds in terms of weather. But you mentioned New Mexico earlier. Where were you there?"

"Albuquerque and Santa Fe. But it was in Santa Fe that I showed that picture of John to people at a couple of trucking companies. One of the truckers recognized him, but said his name was Evan Williams, and the guy in the office who schedules and sends out the drivers agreed, but said he had left for Portland and Seattle three days earlier. He had already off-loaded the cargo he had carried to Portland and gone north, was probably making his second stop, in Seattle, pretty much as we spoke."

"Interesting," I commented. "Was one of the office guys in Santa Fe called Butch?"

"Yes," she said. "The one in the office, a really nice man who told me John had driven the truck for their company to Portland and Seattle. How did you know?"

"He's an old friend of mine," I told her, thinking back to the last time I had talked to Butch Stringer on the phone, as we periodically keep in touch. It had been too long and I reminded myself that I should call him sometime soon.

I met Butch on the Alaskan Highway several years earlier, on my way north to Homer in the spring after spending the winter in the Southwest. He had suffered a horrible accident in purposely driving his Peterbilt cab and trailer rig off the road to avoid hitting a passenger car and a pickup towing a boat, and had been badly injured as a result. It had taken him out of distance driving and put him in the office of a trucking company.

I didn't go into all of that with Amy.

"What did you do when you knew John, or Evan Williams as they knew him, was already gone?" I asked her instead.

"Well, knowing his destination, I caught the first plane I could to Seattle, but when I got there he had left the truck and vanished again. I checked out a few cheap hotels nearby, but no one remembered or recognized him from the picture."

"He does look quite different in the picture," I commented. "Younger, professional, not like a trucker at all."

"I know, but it's the only picture I've had. I knew that he must have found a way to forge the identification that he needed with a more current picture, but I had to use what I had. When he started doing long-haul trucking he started using Evan Williams and had the identification to prove it. It must have tweaked his sense of humor. I imagine him just walking into the nearest liquor store when he wanted a new alias and taking one from whatever whiskey bottle he found first, or that appealed to him."

I had to smile at that idea, knowing John had exhibited a sense of humor that would support that supposition, and also that I had done somewhat the same in collecting names from the bottles of that same kind of alcohol in my own liquor store.

Amy had finished her tea and set the mug down on the table at her end of the sofa.

She yawned, hiding it politely behind her hand.

I glanced at the clock. It was almost midnight.

"Past time for bed, I think," I told her.

Stretch lifted his head, recognizing the word *bed*, stood up and—I have to say it—stretched.

I got up, collected the mugs, and took them to the kitchen sink. He followed and Amy followed him.

"Would you mind if I took a shower in the morning, Maxie?"

"Not at all. Help yourself whenever you wake up."

"Thank you for asking me to stay," she said.

"Anytime," I told her. "We'll call Trooper Nelson in the morning. Go ahead up, if you want. I'll be right behind you."

She said good night and went.

I checked to make sure the doors were securely locked and that I had turned off the outside light over the step, then followed her, carrying Stretch as usual.

In just a few minutes the house was dark and quiet.

Amy had left her door open a bit, but I shut mine, so Stretch would not go exploring and wake her in the night. He's used to son Joe sleeping there and might assume he would be welcome company.

I was comfortable in my own bed and knowing the house was as secure as it could be, thanks to Lew and the new lock. Still, I had taken the shotgun upstairs with me, just in case, and it lay on the other side of the bed, ready for instant use, but an unusual bed companion.

I stared at the dark ceiling and thought about how determined Amy had been to spend years traveling across the country, searching for her brother, who had eluded her right up until his death. Had he even known she was looking for him? Perhaps not, I decided. How sad.

Interesting that she hadn't asked me any questions about John, but probably she would tomorrow.

Her mention of Santa Fe reminded me again that I wanted to give Butch Stringer a call and I thought about that, closed my eyes, took a deep breath or two, and sleep overcame me almost instantly.

EIGHTEEN

Amy's account of love and loss for both herself and John must have gone deeper than I realized, for I dreamed of my Daniel, as I don't do often and treasure as a gift of time.

He was walking across the yard toward where I was standing on the back deck, a younger Stretch trotting along at his side, small feet a dozen to one in his effort to keep up. Daniel was reaching a hand out toward me with a smile that brought him back so strongly that for once I knew it was a dream and that I would wake before he reached me.

And I did, in the too-early darkness of the morning hours, in a house too quiet to get up. So I lay there on my back for a few minutes with my eyes closed, picturing his smile and how much I had missed it since he passed.

Then, as if he had laid out an arm and offered encouragement and comfort, I rolled over toward what had been his side of the bed and went back to sleep with my hand on his pillow.

When I woke again it was still dark, as the year turned toward the winter solstice in our far north, but I could hear the shower running in the bathroom across the hall, remembered that Amy had asked to use it, and knew it was time to get up.

Stretch gave me an impatient look and went to the door, wanting to get out.

A glance at the clock told me it was shortly after eight, late for me, but we had stayed up late the evening before. So I swung my legs out of bed and, deciding I would shower later, got dressed in the slacks and shirt I had been wearing when I came up to bed.

"Come on, Stretch," I suggested, as I opened the door and picked him up. "Let's go down and I'll let you out, which is what I know you need."

Because dachshunds are so long they have weak backs and are libel to spinal injury in going up or down stairs, so I carried him to the bottom, set him down, let him out the back door, and put some food in his bowl before letting him in again.

It had evidently snowed for much of the night, for everything, including Amy's car, was covered with what looked like two to three inches. The sun had come out thinly and there were patches of blue sky overhead, so I thought the snow would soon melt again.

Homer is warmer than Anchorage and most of the rest of the state, except for the southeast panhandle, so we don't often get snow in huge amounts or on a very regular basis. This is not to say that, when the temperature drops, driving on icy roads is any fun, and we can play bumper cars in slick parking lots as well as anybody anywhere else.

I went to the kitchen to get the coffee going and make us something for breakfast and found myself humming "It's Beginning to Look a Lot Like Christmas" as I put eggs to scramble in the pan with the sausage.

"You sound happy," Amy said, coming to stand across the counter from me.

"Blame it on the snow," I told her. "I'll probably be singing 'Jingle Bells' soon."

"Can I do anything to help?"

"You can set the table," I told her, waving a hand in the direction of the cupboard in which I keep the dishes. "The plates are over there and the silverware is in the drawer below."

I filled a platter with scrambled eggs, sausage, and toast and took it to the table, along with steaming mugs of the fresh coffee and some of Becky's homemade peach jam.

Before sitting down I went across the room and pulled back the curtains covering the sliding glass doors that led to the deck, letting in the light and the view of the bay and mountains beyond.

The table set, Amy came across to stand beside me and look out.

"What a beautiful place to live," she said. "With a scene like that, how could anyone leave?"

"Many don't. The last few years we've had an influx of people moving here. Most come as tourists and decide they want to stay—or at least have a place to come back to for the summer months, as many are snowbirds that go south for the winter. They buy or build houses with views of Kachemak Bay from the bluff above town and property values have soared because of it.

"I'm lucky though. This property was outside the city limits when my first husband, Joe, bought it and built this house. Now it's worth what seems like a small fortune to me."

We went back to the table, soon finished breakfast, and were drinking our second mugs of coffee.

"You know," Amy said thoughtfully, setting hers down. "Last night I told you about my search for John across the country. But I don't know how and when you came to know him here in Alaska. Would you tell me about it?"

I realized that she was right. I had done a lot of listening and almost no talking about my short acquaintance with and limited knowledge of John.

"There isn't much to tell," I assured her. "But I'll tell you what I know."

"How did you meet him?"

"Completely by accident," I told her.

"Stretch and I had gone for a walk on the spit," I began, remembering back to that day of wind and weather coming in from the west. "It looked like rain, so we headed for my car, but Stretch's attention was caught by a man who was sitting at a picnic table, warming his hands on a paper cup of coffee from a restaurant across the street that was still open out of season.

"I got talking with him, introduced myself and Stretch, and he said his name was John Walker, that he had come from Anchorage on the Homer Stage Line, a shuttle that goes back and forth between there and here a couple of times a week, and that he had walked out from town to take a look at the spit.

"In a few minutes it did start to rain, so I offered him a ride back to town and dropped him off at the Driftwood Inn."

"But you saw him again," Amy said.

"Yes. I asked how long he planned to be in town and he said he had planned to go back to Anchorage on the Monday shuttle, but as he thanked me for the ride he said a thing I can't get out of my mind, especially now that he's gone. He told me he liked it here so much that, as he put it—and I quote, *Who knows? I like it here so far—interesting place—friendly people. Maybe I'll decide to spend what's left of my life at the end of the road.*"

She stared at me, eyes wide.

"He actually said: *what's left of my life* and *the end of the road*?" she asked. "What an odd way of putting it."

"Yes, he did. And I thought that, too—even more after I was told that he had killed himself. But I think that's what he meant all along—part of why he came here—as far from anywhere he came from and could get in this country."

"When did you see him again?"

"My son, Joe, had flown up from Seattle for one of his short visits and I had asked a few friends of mine and his to come for dinner that Saturday evening. So, on impulse, I called and invited John to join us and he did. We all enjoyed his quiet company and there was nothing to indicate what he had in mind."

"Was that the last time you saw him?"

"It was, but not his last contact. Sometime in the night before he died, he brought two books he had picked up at one of our local bookstores and left them on my front step, wrapped in plastic, with a note asking me to either keep them or return them to where he had bought them. I thought he had probably caught the early shuttle and was already gone, but that it was a little odd that he didn't leave them at the Driftwood Inn, or the bookstore itself that's just a couple of blocks away. As I told you, this picture of Marty"—I picked it up from where I had left it on the table as I went on—"the woman you say is . . . *was* . . . his wife, was tucked into one of them like a bookmark."

Amy frowned, leaned forward, and looked thoughtfully down into the coffee mug that she was holding between her two hands.

"And he never told you where he was from?" she asked, looking up again.

"No. My son, Joe, asked him and was told he was *from the South*. But, aside from that, he never really talked about himself in any detail at all."

"He had changed a lot," she said slowly. "I wonder—"

"You know," I interrupted, "I'm forgetting that I should call the state troopers' office in Anchor Point and see if I can get ahold of Alan Nelson, so you can talk to him. He needs to know the things you've told me. And he can tell us if they know anything new at the crime lab in Anchorage, where they took his body."

I got up from the table and went to the phone, but there was no dial tone when I picked it up to make the call. I put a finger on the hang-up button and jiggled it a couple of times, but the line remained dead.

"Damn," I swore in frustration. "Must have something to do with heavy new snow on the lines." It was a thing I didn't remember ever happening before, but figured that there's always a first time for just about everything.

I fished my cell phone out of the purse that I had left sitting on the kitchen counter the evening before. But I got no success there, either. Evidently I had inadvertently left it turned on the day before, or not noticed the battery was getting low, because it was also dead.

Hooking it up to the charger I keep handy at the back of the kitchen counter, I left it to absorb new strength and turned to Amy with a question.

"Do you have . . ."

But she was already shaking her head.

"Sorry," she said. "I've been using disposables and need to get a new one."

I thought for a moment. I could do one of two things. Either I could wait for the cell to charge, or I could drive down to the police station in the middle of town and contact Trooper Nelson through them.

I decided on the latter and told Amy what I intended to do.

"Will you mind staying here while I'm gone?" I questioned. "I'll be back in less than half an hour."

"Not at all," she told me. "I'll clean up the breakfast dishes while you're gone."

Leaving Stretch with company, I put on my coat and boots and was out the door five minutes later, forgetting to lock the door behind me until I remembered on the road into town. Knowing Amy was there and that I wouldn't be away long, I decided not to go back, and continued on to the police station.

Once there, I told them about my telephone problems and they called the troopers' office in Anchor Point for me. Trooper Nelson, however, was in Kenai, over ninety miles away, for a meeting of some kind, and wouldn't be back until sometime late that afternoon. I left a message asking him to contact me on my cell phone, which I knew would be charged by the time he called. After thanking the helpful woman in the office at the police station, I went back to my car and headed home.

Pulling into my driveway, I noticed that Amy's car was no longer next to where I parked mine. That puzzled me.

I walked up to the door and found it closed, but unlocked. That worried me.

I went inside and called Stretch, who, to my relief, trotted out from the fireplace side of the big room and gave me a questioning look that clearly meant *Where the heck have you been* and *why did you leave me here?*

Locking the door behind me, I called Amy's name, but got no answer.

The breakfast dishes were still on the table, the pot still keeping what was left of the coffee warm in the kitchen. But her coat was gone from the hook by the door.

Upstairs in Joe's bedroom I found her suitcase also gone and the bed left unmade.

Gone! She had simply disappeared! In a hurry, evidently, knowing I would very shortly be back. Why? And where? But mostly . . . why?

After taking the dishes to the kitchen I refilled my mug with coffee and sat down at the table to think it over.

Near the table was a wastebasket that I kept there for tossing away mail I didn't want to keep, paper napkins, and other such recyclable stuff that I felt guilty putting in the garbage pail under the sink. I glanced into it casually, thinking it needed emptying.

Then I stopped, leaned and picked out several pieces of a familiar photograph that I knew I had not and would not have thrown into it. It had been torn through several times by someone who clearly wanted it destroyed. That someone must have been Amy.

Like a jigsaw puzzle I laid the small pieces carefully together, searching the wastebasket for a couple of missing ones until I found and added them to make the picture complete.

What lay before me on the table was the photo Andy had found in the O'Brian book and given to me—the woman Amy had said was John's wife, Marty.

It simply didn't make sense, unless what Amy had told me the evening before didn't make sense, either.

Did it?

NINETEEN

AMY DID NOT COME BACK THAT DAY, as I thought she might.

I called the telephone company on my partially charged cell phone and a young repairman showed up just after noon and fixed my phones in five minutes.

"All three were unplugged," he said, with a glance that told me he thought I had done it myself and was probably suffering from Alzheimer's at what he considered my advanced age.

I assured him I had not, but was sure that, assuming I had, he chalked that up as proof of his theory.

———————

Trooper Alan Nelson called my cell phone late that afternoon from Kenai before starting back to Anchor Point. Hearing that I had several important things to tell and show him, he asked me to wait until he got there, which would be as soon as possible, and showed up on my doorstep just before seven o'clock.

He came in the door after stomping snow from his boots, hung his coat and hat on a hook by the door, and followed me to the table, taking a long look at the shotgun that I had placed once again on the counter by the door.

"Trouble?" he asked as he sat down and looked down at Stretch, who had come trotting across the room. "Hey there, buddy."

"Trouble prevention," I told him. "You've had a long day. Can I get you something to eat?"

"Thanks, but I grabbed a burger and ate it in the car on the way down," he told me. "A cup of coffee would be welcome though."

I poured him some, added cream when he nodded as I held it up, brought the mug to the table, and sat down facing him.

He directed another nod at the photograph I had carefully taped together while I waited for him to arrive.

"Who is this?" he asked me.

"Supposed to be John's wife," I told him.

"How do you know that? And why did you tear it up?"

"I didn't," I assured him. "I found it in my wastebasket when I came back from the police station, where I called because neither of my phones were working. But let me go back to just after you were last here. You already know that John left a couple of books for me to return to the bookstore, right?"

He did.

"So, I took them back and didn't think any more about it."

"Then what?"

"Well, when the article about his suicide came out in last Wednesday's paper, my phone practically never stopped ringing. You know how gossip spreads like wildfire in this town. So I decided on the spur of the moment to fly up to Anchorage, then went on to visit friends in Wasilla, just to get away for a couple of days. You probably know Alex Jensen, who's a trooper based in Palmer. I stayed with him and his lady, Jessie Arnold."

He nodded that he did.

"I flew back yesterday on Grant's noon flight, and when I got home I found my front door unlocked and open a crack. Checking inside I could tell that someone had stayed here while I was gone—actually slept in my bed. Made me furious—still does. I immediately washed all the linen, not thinking there might be something to identify whoever had slept there.

"Whoever it was must have found the key I kept in the shed by the driveway, because it's missing. So a friend came and replaced the lock on the door for me, bless him."

"Notice anything else?"

"Yes. There were a few things moved from where I keep them—a plant, kitchen things, a book I had left on the sofa was moved to the fireplace hearth, the television had been moved. I think it was a woman, but am not absolutely sure."

Nelson had taken out a notebook and pen and was taking notes. At that suggestion he paused and held up a hand to stop me.

"What makes you think it was a woman?"

"There was a perfume scent that wasn't mine in the bed and in the bathroom—where she used my toothpaste, as a matter of fact. I tossed it out. It was the kind of scent that no guy would use as aftershave—very floral. It's gone down the drain now and the sheets and pillowcases are back on my bed. But I think I'd be able to identify it, if I smelled it again."

"You're probably right," he said, and went back to writing. "Then what?"

"Nothing from that direction. Whoever it was didn't come back, but probably wouldn't have if she saw my car parked here and knew I was home, would she?"

"Not if she had any sense," he said with a grin, giving the shotgun a glance. "But I'm glad to hear you had the lock replaced. Go on."

So I told him about Andy giving me the picture of John's wife, having found it in one of the books.

"And you say you didn't tear it up."

"I didn't. His sister did that, while I was gone to the police station, calling you. Last night she showed up at my door."

"Andy's sister?"

"No. John's."

That stopped Nelson's note taking. He raised his head with a jerk and looked at me, wide-eyed.

"*Really!* How did you know she was his sister?"

"Amy Fletcher is her name. And she told me she was, but she knew so much about him that I believed her. We talked a long time and she told me how she had been following and searching for him since sometime after the Twin Towers fell in New York. He and his wife, Marty, both worked in the second tower. She evidently died in it, like so many others, when it fell. He, obviously, didn't."

"That may explain that belt buckle Stretch found."

"Yes. But I don't understand why Amy disappeared while I was gone to give you a call—or why she tore up this picture. It doesn't make sense to me. She had another picture, one of John when he was younger. There was no mistaking that it was him."

"Amy Fletcher. Was Fletcher her given or married name?"

"She didn't say, but I got the feeling that she was single and it was her maiden name because she's been searching for him by herself for a number of years and didn't mention leaving a husband or family in order to do it. She was picking up jobs as she traveled when she needed to."

Nelson frowned. "Interesting," he said thoughtfully. "Do you know of anything that she may have left prints on? We can now check him out by the name she gave you—Fletcher. But we might find her prints in a search, if we had some."

"I thought back to what Amy had handled. "The mug she drank coffee from this morning is in the dishwasher, but it's only half full, so I haven't run it yet. I'll get it for you."

"Let me, so her prints aren't smudged. You've already handled the mug, so I'll take your prints to eliminate them from the search."

He did both of those things, carefully wrapping the mug in a paper bag to carry to the crime lab, and taking my prints before he left.

I told him everything I could think of that would be of help and he left, pleased with the progress he felt we had made.

"I'll be sure you get the mug back when they finish with it and will let you know if we find out anything new. Please call the number on the card I gave you if that woman, Amy, comes back, or if you find out where she is."

I thanked him and promised I would, then stood in the doorway and gave him a wave as he backed out of the drive onto East End Road and was quickly gone.

———

After feeding Stretch, I ate another bowl of soup and a tuna sandwich for dinner, not wanting to go to the trouble of making anything that required more effort. When I finished, I rinsed out the bowl and spoon I had used and set them in the dish drainer beside the sink.

It had been a stressful couple of days and I could feel a headache coming on, so I took some Tylenol and went to have a lie-down on the sofa, after building a small fire in the fireplace.

Stretch watched from where he was on the hearth rug and laid his head back down when he saw me settle with a light blanket over me. As he grows older he naps more and isn't as active as he was in the past. But isn't that true for us all?

As I dozed off, I wondered again fleetingly why Amy had left in such a hurry. It didn't seem much like what I had learned of and from her, but then how much did I actually know about her anyway?

I was asleep in minutes, refusing to wear myself out with more speculation on the past week's events and puzzles, good or bad.

I wound up sleeping there all night.

It was still dark when I woke, disoriented and yawning, wondering what time it was.

That time of year, when it gets dark earlier in the afternoon and stays dark until later the following morning, it's difficult to tell the time by the amount of light and dark, so we Alaskans do a lot of clock-watching. Having spent the last few winters in the southwestern states, where it gets dark later and light earlier, I was still feeling a bit out of sync and found myself taking naps at odd times.

I got up, took a look at the clock, and, finding it was five thirty in the morning, went straight back to sleep for another couple of hours.

When I finally woke for good at just after seven o'clock, I felt much better. I let Stretch out and back in, then fed him before going upstairs, where I took a long, hot shower, washed my hair, brushed my teeth, and felt ready for whatever the rest of the day might bring, hopefully something good and ordinary.

I have never suffered from underconfidence, you understand.

TWENTY

PEACE AND QUIET WERE A GOODLY PART OF THAT MORNING. I made and ate breakfast as I watched the rising sun make sparkles on the waters of the bay and gild the mountaintops on the other side.

Clean, well rested, and ready to take on whatever the day might have to offer, I found my outlook had shifted, as it often does when I stop focusing too much on anything or one side of a question. I told myself to stop worrying about defending my territory from an unknown someone who had trespassed, though I still wondered why they had picked my house in particular.

With no way of answering that question, I decided to let it go completely for the moment. My defense had confined me to my house, however much I valued it and resented the intrusion. Was I going to allow myself to be a prisoner of my own worries and anger, or not? I resolved that I was not.

I would take Stretch and leave the house—go somewhere else for a while.

I would have headed for another of my walks on the beach of the spit, but had no desire to wade through snow and knew it wouldn't be any fun at all for my low-slung dachshund.

Then I remembered that I had forgotten to pick up the mail on my way back from the airport on Sunday and that became my goal for the moment.

First I went around and made sure that the doors to the deck and windows were locked and noticed that in the sunshine the snow was beginning to melt and drip off the roof. I put on a warm coat, boots, and gloves, and used one of the new keys to lock the front door as I went out.

Stretch, wearing his red sweater, I carried to the car, so he wouldn't get his feet wet, and deposited him in his basket.

I backed out of the drive and headed for the post office, where I found a handful of mail waiting in my box—several bills, two mail-order catalogues, and a Hallmark card from Sharon. In bright colors it read:

> *No one ever said that life was easy.*
> *Well, someone may have said it.*
> *Someone dumb.*

She had added a note to say that it matched her mood of the moment as she hadn't realized just how much stuff they would want to take along in their temporary move to Portland, that they were both busy packing, but would call me soon.

Good choice, Joe, I thought, not for the first time. She has a healthy sense of humor and I'm going to enjoy having her as a daughter-in-law.

From the post office I headed to the grocery store that is almost next door, where I parked, and left Stretch in the car once again. There I picked out a small pork roast to put in the oven for dinner and added a couple of baking potatoes to my cart, along with a jar of applesauce, and some greens and tomatoes for a salad. Living alone, I seldom do much baking anymore, so I went to the bakery for half a chocolate cake that I knew from past experience would be an indulgent dessert addition.

Having paid for the groceries, I was looking over the rack of new movies for rent in the front of the store when someone laid a hand on my shoulder.

"Hey," said a familiar voice, and I turned to find Harriet Christianson smiling at me.

"You're home again, I see. Tried to call you the end of last week, but all I got was your machine. You missed a good evening with the quilting ladies. They were disappointed when you didn't show."

"Oh, Harriet," I said, remembering the quilting party I had skipped out on in order to get away to Anchorage. "Will next meeting do?"

"Of course," she told me. "We'd love to see your treasures anytime you can make it. Did you have a good trip?"

"I did. I got a little Christmas shopping done and had a two-day visit with some old friends."

We talked a little longer before I took my groceries out to the car, where Stretch was watching the people coming and going. I put the sacks in the backseat before returning the cart.

"With this melting snow it's a bad day for a walk, lovie," I told him as I slid in behind the wheel. "How about we stay warm and dry in the car and just take a drive out to the end of the spit and back?"

He never disagrees.

So that's what we did. We stopped in a pull off to watch the tide slowly coming in from Cook Inlet, splashing its lacy edges up a little farther with each wave. The beach was empty of people, except for one lone walker who I didn't recognize. He was strolling along with his hands in his pockets, cap flaps pulled down around his ears, rubber boots on his feet.

I watched him go casually out for a walk, snow or no snow, though the incoming salt water was doing its best to melt and erase as much as it could reach, wave by wave, each a little higher than the last.

We drove back to town and on impulse I pulled in to Ulmer's to pick up some red, white, and green yarns, thinking that, as she and Joe were coming for Christmas, I'd knit Sharon a stocking to match the one I made for him years ago when he was small. I could use it as a pattern if I could find where I had packed it away with the holiday decorations and ornaments in the attic.

It would be a good project to keep my hands busy in the next week or two. I decided that I'd go up soon, find it and my knitting needles, and make a start.

I took Stretch in with me. A couple of the clerks who work there are friends of his and don't mind if I bring him in on his leash. They also usually have a treat or two saved for him, which he expects and accepts as his due.

I took my time in the yarn department, picked out the colors I wanted, and had started for the checkout counter when I was side-tracked by the puzzles and games selection. Not finding anything new or tempting, I decided to give my friend Becky a call and see if she'd like to come for dinner and a game or two of Farkel. Lew was an avid game player and would probably also enjoy an evening that included a meal he didn't have to make for himself.

"Time to go home and get ourselves some lunch," I told Stretch, as we started for the car. "Then I'm going to call Becky and Lew and we'll make a cheerful evening of it."

———————

They both happily accepted my invitation.

"I'll bring the wine this time," Becky told me.

———————

"Something smells delicious," Lew, arriving first, said as he hung his coat by the door. "Any more trouble with unwanted houseguests?"

"Nary a one," I told him. "Thanks to your assistance with the new lock, I've managed to keep them at bay. But actually none have shown up at all."

"Good," he said, and assured me once again, "You've got my number if they do."

———————

Becky followed him closely. So we had time for a glass of the wine she had brought along and conversation around the fireplace before dinner.

"So Joe and Sharon have decided to tie the knot finally," she said. "Harriet Christianson told me when I stopped at the library the other day. How about having it tied out on Niqa Island?"

"Great idea," I agreed. "She suggested that to me a few days back and I was going to ask you about it before I said anything to Joe and Sharon. Do you think it would be okay with the rest of your family?"

"Sure. But I'll check if you like and you can let me know what dates they pick."

———

The dinner turned out well and we had the cake with ice cream for dessert, which especially pleased Lew, as he is a chocolate lover.

Then I cleared the table and got out the Farkel board and the box of the dice required to play.

It's an addictive game and we played four rounds, two of which Lew won, to his delight, but it's all in the numbers you can roll with the dice that add up as you count and move your piece around the board. Sometimes they fall your way, sometimes not, and you get left behind while someone else makes it all the way to the finish line.

By the time we had played four rounds and the bottle of wine was empty, we were about ready to call it a night.

"Time to head for the barn," Lew said. "Thanks for asking me, Maxie. Don't forget to give me a call if you have any more trouble."

I told him I wouldn't, waved to him from the door, and went back to toss a log on the dying fire and sit down with Becky for a few minutes.

"What trouble?" she immediately asked me.

I told her about finding that someone had stayed uninvited in my house while I was gone to Anchorage and Wasilla.

"Good grief! Did you call the police?"

"Not right away, no. But Lew came and changed the lock on my front door, which gives me confidence that whoever it was won't be able to get in so easily again. Also, I'm leaving my shotgun within easy reach these days. So don't worry. The police know now and I live closer than most people to the station, so they could be here quickly if I had to call."

"Well, promise me you'll take care," she said. "And remember that you can come and stay with me if you want to."

"Thanks. I'll keep that in mind," I assured her, as I had assured Lew.

It's really great to have good friends who treat you almost like family. Sometimes I think it says more than that, actually. Good friends make a choice in helping or taking you in. Family can't.

TWENTY-ONE

THE NEXT MORNING AFTER BREAKFAST I gave another thought to finding Joe's Christmas stocking in the attic.

"Come along," I called to Stretch. "You can come up with me while I search the attic for the Christmas trunk."

I carried him up and was surprised to find the door at the end of the second-story hall not standing open, but not closed tightly either.

I couldn't remember when I had last been up there, but the attic isn't heated, so I always close the door to keep the cold out. I carefully closed it behind me and carried Stretch up the stairs.

Like most attics, through the years it had become a repository for odds and ends that are somehow precious, are too good to get rid of, or are seldom used. Christmas ornaments, for example, have a specific, once-a-year purpose and spend the rest of it waiting for the holiday to roll around again. Under one small window I have a trunk full of things I have collected over the years that have meaning to me: my high school and college annuals and diplomas; letters

I want to keep from people I have known and valued; the birth certificates of my two children, son Joe and my daughter, who lives on the East Coast. And there are other miscellaneous items that mean something only to me—and a few things I have forgotten why I wanted to keep, but never seem to find the time or inclination to sort and discard.

Sometime in the summer I had gone up to the attic, then even farther up a steep stair that is almost a ladder on one side of that under-the-eves space, pushed open a narrow door overhead, and stepped out onto the small, flat part of the roof my husband Joe had built. About ten feet square, it is a widow's walk with a decorative, waist-high railing—like the ones he had grown up seeing on the Northeast coast, where wives watched for their husbands' fishing boats to come back safely from the sea. Those that never saw them come home must have walked nervously back and forth in the small space, and given rise to the name for this type of outlook. I don't think there's another like it anywhere else in Homer—maybe even in Alaska.

This time I didn't go up that far, however, as I was looking for the trunk that contained our family's traditional Christmas decorations, which were most precious and irreplaceable. There I thought I would find son Joe's hand-knit stocking to use as a pattern for the one I intended to make for Sharon.

Looking across the attic to a space under a small window, I saw it, as expected, with a box or two of Christmas tree lights lying on top. Winding my way through the odd bits and pieces of our lives through the years—a chair with a broken rocker, a pile of motor-cycle books a younger Joe had collected, a clear plastic bag holding my daughter's dolls and the stuffed animals that had filled more of her bed than she did as a child, a few framed and now dusty family pictures I had no room for on the walls downstairs, a filing cabinet that held I wasn't sure what, old tax records probably, but wasn't about to find out on this particular day—I came at last to the south side of the attic and the trunk I was aiming for.

Inside, under a pile of unused, leftover holiday cards, I found Joe's stocking, took it out, and closed the lid again before turning back toward the stairs.

On the other side of the attic I could hear Stretch scratching and growling at something against the west wall, so I took a different route through the attic collection to see what he was worrying, hoping he hadn't found a mouse.

A stack of cardboard boxes lay between us. I walked around them and what I saw there on the floor stopped me cold.

An old carpet I had once used in front of the fireplace downstairs, rolled up and put next to the attic wall several years earlier, had now been pulled out and lay, more loosely rolled, in the space in front of me. Stretch had been pulling on its closest end, enough to partially unroll part of it. From the end closest to me a foot protruded—a woman's foot, in a plain brown businesslike shoe with a low heel—a shoe I didn't recognize.

I caught my breath and stood staring at it in total surprise and shock for a long minute.

Then I stepped forward, snatched up Stretch to keep him from any more tugging on the carpet than he had already done, and though he wiggled and whined to be put down, I took him down the stairs to the bedroom level.

"Stay," I told him, and, closing the door firmly to keep him out, went back up to the attic.

There I hesitated. Should I or should I not unroll the carpet to find out if the person inside it was really as dead as I believed? I reached out cautiously and laid my fingers on the ankle above the shoe. It was as cold as the rest of the attic, which was cooler than the rest of the house, but not freezing cold, as some of the household heat creeps in under the door and up the stairs, and the fireplace chimney rises through it in the southeast corner, adding a little warmth.

It was pretty clear that whoever the woman was, she was no longer alive.

That observation decided me to leave things as they were, ignore my curiosity to know who it was, and go back downstairs to call law enforcement.

I picked up Stretch on the way down and called Trooper Nelson in Anchor Point, who said he would be there as soon as he could drive to Homer, but also that I should call the local police.

I did that, then sat down at the table with the cold half cup of coffee I had left there to await their arrival as I wondered who this dead person was and who had left her in my attic—possibly the same person who had stayed in my house while I was away?

If I hadn't decided to knit Sharon a Christmas stocking and gone up to find Joe's, it would have been at least a month before I went up to retrieve the holiday decorations.

How long had I been sleeping in the room pretty much right under her and how long would I have gone on doing so if not for that stocking?

It gave me the shudders.

Two sips of cold coffee later the police were knocking on my door.

I showed them up the stairs and into the attic where the body lay wrapped in the carpet, told them how I had found it, and said that I had no idea who it was. Then I went back downstairs to wait for Alan Nelson, who showed up a few minutes later.

"Who is it?" he asked me as he came in the door.

"I don't know," I told him. "She's rolled into an old carpet and I didn't unroll it, though Stretch had pulled at it a bit. I left her as I found her and brought him down to call you. I wouldn't even have known she was there if I hadn't heard him growling and gone to see what he was after in that far corner of the attic."

"Why did you go up there?"

I told him why and showed him the Christmas stocking I had gone to retrieve, which now lay on the table along with the yarn from Ulmer's and my knitting needles.

"Well, I need to go on up," he said. "And you'd better come with me to see if you can identify this person. There must be a reason she's been left in your attic, mustn't there? So it may be someone you know."

That thought didn't appeal to me at all. I had wondered about it before his suggestion and was hoping against hope that it was not.

So I left Stretch downstairs in the office, with the door securely shut so he couldn't follow us, and went up as requested.

We reached the top of the stairs and stepped into the attic. Across the space between us the three policemen were gathered around the rug, which they had unrolled to uncover the body that had been wrapped inside. All three of them turned and recognized Trooper Nelson with nods.

He stepped forward and took a long, frowning look at the body, then turned back to me.

"Mrs. McNabb," he said formally, "would you take a look and see if you can identify this woman as someone you know?"

The four men moved aside to leave room for me to step forward and see her clearly. Taking a deep breath, I walked the few steps required to reach the space where the dead woman now lay on her back, arms at her sides, at one end of the carpet in which she had been wrapped.

For a long moment, as they waited, I stood silent at her feet and stared at the pale face that was streaked with blood from a bullet hole in the right temple. It had run into her hair and left a significant stain on the carpet that had concealed her identity.

I slowly realized that I had somehow half expected the body to be that of the disappearing Amy Fletcher. And I suppose that I might have understood her having followed her brother John in suicide. But there was no gun and she couldn't have wrapped her own body in that heavy piece of carpet, so someone else had to have killed and left her there in my attic.

But it was not Amy.

To my astonishment and confused shock, it was the woman who had flown with me on the plane to Anchorage, whom I had seen again in the Hilton Hotel lobby, and thought I might have seen a third time in Wasilla as we left the bookstore.

I turned toward Trooper Nelson, who had moved to stand at my side. I must have turned white because he was holding my elbow, as if afraid I might faint.

"You do recognize her, don't you?" he asked quietly.

"Yes. I don't know her name or anything about her, never talked to her, but I think she was following me when I flew to Anchorage last week. I saw her clearly twice—once here as we both boarded the Grant Aviation plane and once in Anchorage in the lobby of the Hilton Hotel, where I stayed for one night—possibly once again, later, in Wasilla, as my friend Jessie and I left a bookstore in a small mall there. But I'm not sure about that because when I looked again she was not to be seen, so I could be mistaken."

But somehow I knew I was not and wondered why in the world she had simply lurked about where I could see her and not come to speak to me.

Maybe I was wrong and just imagining things.

At that point Trooper Nelson suggested that we go downstairs to call and wait for a van to transport the woman's body. So that's what we did.

Two of the policemen left to report to the station, leaving the third, Lanny Toliver, with Trooper Nelson to hear and record whatever I could tell them.

I put on a fresh pot of coffee and we sat around my table to drink it as we talked.

The young policeman flipped open the notebook he carried and asked the first question.

"There's no identification on the woman at all—no purse and nothing in the pockets of her slacks. So we have no way of knowing who she is. But you say she took the same plane to Anchorage that you did? What day was that, and which flight?"

I told him that it had been the nine o'clock flight on Wednesday of the preceding week.

"Good," said Trooper Nelson, rising from the table. "I can check on who she is through the Grant Aviation records. May I use your phone?"

"Certainly," I told him.

"But you never spoke to her? Just noticed her on the plane and at the hotel?" asked the policeman.

"That's right. She sat across the aisle and one row ahead of me on the plane. Then she was sitting in the lobby of the Hilton Hotel when I went through on my way to do some shopping."

"And you're sure you don't know who she is?"

I assured him I didn't, and that I had never spoken to her.

As the policeman wrote down my answers, Trooper Nelson returned to the table with a frown of hesitation and confusion on his face. He sat down and gave me a long, thoughtful look before telling us what he had learned. Somehow I knew I was not going to like hearing it.

"The Grant Aviation ticket records say that the driver's license she showed them was current and issued in New York City," he said slowly. "The picture on it matched the face of the dead woman upstairs, who bought the ticket . . . and the name . . ."

He hesitated a second and gave me another perplexed and questioning look before continuing.

"The name was . . . Amy Fletcher."

TWENTY-TWO

It was so unexpected and startling that I froze there at the table, eyes wide, mouth open.

"But . . . But . . . ," I sputtered. Then I caught a breath. "That can't be right."

"I think it is," he said. "And there is more than one way we can find out—through records in that state, for a start. Did you ever see identification from the woman who said she was Amy Fletcher? The woman who stayed with you here?"

I shook my head. "One doesn't usually ask for identification from houseguests, does one?"

At that point the young policeman, who was listening carefully, got up from the table to meet the other two who were coming in the door with a stretcher, having returned with a van.

"Take notes for me, Alan, will you?" he asked.

"Sure. We'll go over them later."

"Wait just a minute, Lanny," I said to him. "How's your father? I heard he's been ill."

"He's doing fine now," he said, turning back with a smile. "Thanks for asking. Got his medication mixed up and it put him in the hospital for a night or two. He's okay now."

"Tell him I asked, will you?"

"Will do."

Homer really is a small town.

I watched him walk past us and disappear up the stairs, following the other two on their way to the attic.

"Will they take her to Anchorage?" I asked, wondering about the woman they were about to carry down.

"Yes, to the crime lab, like John," he told me. Then he turned back to the notes he was taking.

"And everything this woman who stayed here told you about herself and John Walker—Fletcher, perhaps—seemed credible?" he asked.

"Yes. She knew things about him—and his wife, Marty. What she told me was completely possible—and plausible."

"Interesting. She must have known both of them before—in New York."

"But why would the woman who came here—stayed here with me when I invited her—tell me she was Amy Fletcher, John's sister, if she wasn't—isn't?"

"I don't know, but she must have her own pretty strong reasons for impersonating Amy," he said thoughtfully.

"Maybe that's why she disappeared so fast when I went to the police station to have them call you because my phones weren't working—they were dead. But there was nothing wrong with them when the repairman checked them later. They had all three been unplugged, and now I'm thinking it must have been by her. But she and everything she had brought in with her was gone when I came back about half an hour later. And the photograph I showed you had been torn up and tossed in the wastebasket. I don't understand that at all."

"Could something about it have made her angry?"

I thought about it briefly, shrugged, then turned to his next question.

"You said you haven't seen her since."

"No, I haven't. I thought at first she might come back, but she hasn't, so I let it go."

He frowned. "It makes me think that, whoever she is, she didn't want to have to identify or explain herself to law enforcement. It reinforces the idea that she also may have been responsible for the death of the woman in your attic."

That was a sobering thought.

"I spoke with the crime lab this morning," he told me after a moment's thoughtful pause. "They are under the impression that Walker—or Fletcher, if that's who he turns out to be—possibly didn't kill himself after all. The fingerprints on the gun are his, but it had been carefully cleaned, inside and out, before it was used that last time and placed in his hand. And there are too few on it for him to have carried and handled it without that cleaning, just enough to make it ostensible that he shot himself with it. Who would bother to clean a gun they were going to use for that purpose?"

"So you're thinking that she may have shot him, right?"

"I'm thinking one of them did and it makes more sense that it wasn't that one," he said, waving a hand in the direction of the stretcher that had been brought down from the attic and was now being carried out my door by two of the policemen. The third followed closely with the bloody carpet, now rolled up again. "She at least was making no secret of who she was, was she? At least it seems pretty clear, but we'll verify it, of course."

"You're telling me a lot of things I wouldn't expect to hear," I suggested.

"Yes, that's right," Nelson said. "But I've learned a lot from what you've told me and I want you to know as much of this as I can."

"Why? My impression of law enforcement officers is that they keep most of what they do and learn to themselves."

"Well, that's correct and not correct. It depends on the situation. We don't share details that may compromise a case we're working unless it's necessary. That's true. But you can understand that there are reasons behind it."

"You don't want what you know to reach the people you're investigating, I suppose."

"Right again. But there are times when keeping things—details and problems—to ourselves actually makes it more dangerous to innocent people and, perhaps, to us as well. I think this is one of those times—for you."

"Why?" I asked again, suddenly feeling vulnerable in a way I hadn't before. If someone else thought I was at risk, then it would behoove me to think so, too.

"Because you're obviously an intelligent and observant woman, who's pretty accepting of people and what they do, as long as it's not threatening to anyone, including yourself, but who takes things as they come and makes pretty good decisions about them."

"Thank you," I said. "I'd like to think that's true. But I'm as fallible as the next person in line."

"Aren't we all?" He grinned.

———————

Did I happen to mention that I really like State Trooper Alan Nelson?

———————

His next question startled me again, as he glanced across the room and his grin faded.

"Have you checked that shotgun since she left?"

It lay where I had kept it handy, on the kitchen counter by the door.

"No. Should I have?"

"Let's take a look," he said, rising to pick up the shotgun and bring it back to the table.

There he broke it open so we could both take a look at the shells with which I had loaded it.

They were gone. The gun was empty.

Aside from holding it by the barrel and beating someone over the head with the stock, there was no way it would provide protection at all. And no one was going to allow me to get close enough to do that. Particularly someone we both were now certain had unloaded and made it useless as a defense, who would now think that it was no threat.

"She must have collected what was hers, torn up the photo, and gone out the door in a hurry," he observed. "But she took the time to unload this gun before she left. And that tells me it's probable that she means to come back."

"Why ever would she want to do that?" I asked. "If it were me, and I'd killed two people at the end of the road in Homer, Alaska, I'd take the first plane out of Anchorage to the Lower Forty-eight and lose myself in some big city in the very middle of the United States. Maybe even fly out to Europe or Asia."

"You," he reminded me, "are not a stone-cold killer with an obsession to kill not only two people, but anyone who gets in her way, or who knows what she looks like, are you? If I were you, I'd let me drive you to Anchorage and put you on the first plane out of there to anywhere. I'd take your own advice and get lost somewhere she would never, ever think of looking for you.

"For she would look. Never doubt it. If she has gone to the trouble of tracing both John and his sister, Amy, for years, all the way across the country and up to Alaska, to kill them both, she'd look for you, too. And she's not only gotten good at it. She's a chameleon—changes into whoever, whatever she feels will convince people that her truth is worth paying attention to, taking care of. She had you fooled. And you're the only person who can identify her, right?"

As I thought about that, something cold turned over in my stomach, for I believed he was right and I was that person. But it also made me very, very angry. To be forced out of my own home—to run from the place where I grew up and belonged—was not only intolerable, it was ludicrous.

I shook my head as I looked up at him.

"No," I told him stubbornly. "I've never run from anything in my life and won't now. I'd be always looking over my shoulder—

living in fear—unless I got complacent and made mistakes that would get me killed. I won't do that—can't. It's just not the way I'm wired."

We looked at each other and each took a deep breath as he sat back down, the shotgun between us on the table.

He shook his head and grinned.

"I wouldn't either," he said. "I understand that *wired* bit. I didn't think you would and I couldn't, either. So let's figure out what we can do, for I can't stay here to stand guard, you know, however much I'd like to. She'd find a way around or through me if she knew I was here. So, if she's watching, she's got to see me leave.

"Now, where are some new shells for this shotgun?"

TWENTY-THREE

By THE TIME TROOPER ALAN NELSON left my house it was dark outside, but we had a plan that was as good as we could make it and had implemented parts of it.

"We're not going to think that it's possible that she may come back," he had told me. "We're going to proceed believing that she will—and soon. But I think that now we're as ready for her as we can be."

We were almost right in that assumption.

"She may be watching the house," he said, as he got up from the table, where we had worked out and agreed on strategy. "If she is, I want her to see me leave. But I'm going to spend the night here in town at the police station. So I'll be minutes away. I've added my cell phone number to your cell's list, so you must keep it close—in a pocket would be best. I'll do the same with mine. Anything happens—she shows up—you don't let her in. You call me, right?"

"Right!"

"You don't have to say anything if she's where she can hear you. Just put it through and I'll wait a second or two to listen. If you don't say anything to me, I'll know that she's there and listening, too. Then I won't say anything because she might hear my voice on your phone. I'll just come—fast—while you keep her talking."

It sounded good to me and reasonable.

"And don't forget to keep that shotgun within hand's reach if you possibly can."

As if . . . I thought.

I walked him to the door, thanked him as he stepped out through it, and watched for a minute as he walked down the drive to his car.

"Lock that door," he called before climbing in, starting the engine, and beginning to back out of the drive.

"You've got nothing to worry about there," I said under my breath, closed it, and did as he said.

———

Then I walked slowly around the spaces that made up that first floor of my house, looking again to make sure everything was in the order we had decided on. It looked completely normal, but he had helped me pull closed all the curtains and blinds on the windows and doors, so no one could peer in from outside.

We had left several lights on that I normally turned off when I settled by the fireplace for the evening: the ones over the kitchen sink and dining table, the one I always turned on to read, one across from it next to the television. I left both the television and radio turned off, abandoning my usual music for the ability to hear clearly. Everything seemed in order.

Stretch raised his head from where he had been napping on the rug by the fire I had kindled earlier. He watched me carry the shot-gun across the room, lay it on the floor beside the sofa, and sit down in my usual place before returning to his snooze. I knew he would hear faster than I would if anyone came close to our house—my early-warning system.

I sat looking at him, hearing him snore softly, and thinking how quickly he was growing older. Weren't we both? But one day not so long from now he would pass. What would I do without him? But I had always imagined that he would simply go to wherever Daniel waited; he would be as glad to have his dog's good company as I hoped he would mine, when it was my turn. So my being left behind would be their gain, and that idea, loving them both, pleased me, though I already knew how lonely I would be without them.

How little we know of death. What's left behind physically is just a shell of a person and we have no way of knowing what comes after, if anything. Memory is really all that's left, isn't it? We keep a few familiar things that are precious to us for a myriad of reasons, but mostly because they remind us of whatever we want or need to remember.

But considering death shouldn't be part of the current equation, I decided. It wasn't helpful.

Settling back, I left my shoes on the floor and lifted my legs onto the sofa, gaining a slightly different perspective on what lay around me, familiar, yet somehow newly seen under the current circumstances. A lot of my living space and the things in it I took for granted and seldom really looked at. Now wasn't the time for that, I decided.

———————

I heard a car pass on East End Road at the far end of my driveway, had been hearing them, but not consciously marking the familiar background sound of tires on asphalt. My driveway is not paved, so I knew I would hear the sound of tires on gravel if a car turned into it. Shortly after that what was probably a pickup went by, going in the same eastward direction, for something in the bed of it rattled.

Giving up listening, I picked up my book and tried to read, but it had been a long and stressful day and I grew a little drowsy.

———————

Then, suddenly, I was wide-awake, sitting straight up and listening hard.

There had been a sound. And it hadn't come from outside. It had come from somewhere inside the house: a very soft sound, but definitely inside somewhere.

Listening hard, I didn't move, waiting to hear it again.

Nothing.

You're being paranoid, I told myself, deciding it was probably just one of those aged-house sounds you become so used to that you don't even hear them except once in a while as familiar and comforting background music.

But I didn't go back to drowsing, either, though I relaxed enough to lean back.

Stretch had raised his head as I sat up abruptly. Now he laid it down again and closed his eyes.

I had to smile. If there had been anything unusual, he would have heard it, too, wouldn't he? I considered, as I had been doing for the last few months, that maybe he was growing a little deaf in his advanced years. On our next trip to the vet I would have to remember to mention it to her.

Maybe some coffee would help keep me awake, I thought. I went across to the kitchen, where I poured a mug half full of the cold coffee in the pot, put it in the microwave, and waited for it to heat as I watched it go around inside.

It must have been the hum of that handy kitchen appliance that covered any small sound she made as she came down the stairs and into the room behind me, for I didn't hear her. But, as the microwave finished its work and the hum subsided, I did hear Stretch growl warningly, as he would to an unknown or uninvited stranger that he considered an invasion of his space and, therefore, threatening to himself and me.

Mug in my hand, I turned around to see the woman who had called herself Amy Fletcher standing there, halfway between the sofa and the kitchen, between Stretch and me. She held my shotgun with one hand, having picked it up from the floor where I had left it. In the other she had a small, nasty-looking black handgun, and it was pointed directly at me.

I didn't move.

Idiot, I thought, as I stared at her. *You forgot to bring the shotgun with you.*

"So . . . ," she said. "You and that trooper have made a *plan* to lure me out, have you? So he can show up like a white knight and ride to your rescue, right?"

I didn't answer. How could she have known that? How had she gotten into my house, for another matter?

The doors were still shut and locked, the curtains carefully drawn closed over locked windows.

Several questions filled my mind.

"Who are you?" I asked first.

She smiled—a nasty, self-satisfied, taunting sort of smile that I thought went rather well with her nasty little gun.

"All in good time," she told me. "First you will sit down in that chair at the table where you two hatched your worthless plan. Do it!" she snapped when I didn't move immediately, and gestured with the gun.

I moved slowly to a place at the table that faced her and the room and sat, setting the half cup of coffee in front of me.

"Pull the chair close to the table, put both your hands on it, and don't even think about moving," she told me. "I'm going to get rid of this useless item," she said, lifting the shotgun a few inches to show me, "that your trooper so carefully reloaded."

How could she possibly have known that?

Keeping me in sight by moving sideways, she went across to the door that opened onto the deck, and pushed aside the covering curtain. To move the dead bolt that would unlock the door, she had to move the shotgun and hold it under the other arm. After doing that, she turned her attention momentarily from me to what she was doing, allowing me those few seconds unobserved, in which I took the risk of slipping a quick hand into the pocket of my slacks and pressing the button on the cell phone that would open the connection with Trooper Nelson. By the time she turned back I once again had both hands on top of the table.

She slid the door open and tossed the shotgun out without looking after it. I heard it hit the deck hard before she closed and locked the door again, pulled the curtains, and moved back into the room.

Stretch growled again, on his feet now, not moving from the rug in front of the fireplace, but ready.

She gave him a glance.

"Make him stop that, or I will," she told me, and pointed the handgun in his direction. "Do it!"

"Can I call him over here, please?"

"No. What you will do is get up slowly, take him into your office there, leave him inside and close the door so he can't get out. Now! Move!"

I did what she told me, though Stretch—who's no dummy—had already concluded by her tone in speaking to me that she was some kind of threat, and wasn't happy at all about being shut out behind a door he had no way of opening. It deprived him of his assumed right as protector, but gave me a hint of relief that he wouldn't be hurt or killed in whatever happened next.

I could hear him scratching at the door and whining.

"Now what?" I asked her, firmly checking again to be sure the door was tightly closed. "And who are you, by the way? I know you're not Amy Fletcher. And why kill her?"

"What makes you think I did?"

"Pretty obvious, isn't it? But first, who are you anyway?"

If I could keep her talking long enough, I knew Alan Nelson would show up somehow. But he wouldn't be able to get in, would he? All the doors were locked.

"How did you get in here?" I asked before she could answer, if she intended to.

She didn't. Instead, she once again gave me that self-satisfied smile—a crocodile smile, I thought, and out of nowhere remembered Lewis Carroll.

How doth the little crocodile
Improve his shining tail,
And pour the waters of the Nile
On every golden scale!

How cheerfully he seems to grin!
How neatly spread his claws,
And welcomes little fishes in
With gently smiling jaws!

How well it suited her.

TWENTY-FOUR

"GO UP THE STAIRS," SHE TOLD ME with a twitch of the gun barrel in that direction.

"Why?"

"For me to know and you to find out," she said angrily. "Go. Just remember that I'll be right behind you."

Slowly I went up until I reached the landing at the top, with its hallway that led past three bedrooms and the bath, to the far end.

There I hesitated, wondering if I could turn fast enough to catch her off guard and push her back down the stairs without getting shot.

Glancing back, I saw that she was not in reach behind me, but three steps down—waiting.

"Go on to the end of the hall."

I did and stood before the door to the attic.

"What now?"

"Open the door and go up," she said.

As I opened it and stared ahead into the dark, narrow stairwell that led to the attic, I thought of the body found earlier in the day rolled into the carpet and cast into a corner. There were a couple more old carpets there. Perhaps . . .

My breathing changed and for the first time real fear flooded in with adrenaline. I could feel my heart beating hard and fast in my chest.

I knew—did not guess, but knew—that this woman meant to kill and leave me, as she had left the real Amy Fletcher, in my own attic.

"Why?" I asked her.

"Because I said to. Go."

With no choice left but to die either there in the hallway or up in the attic, I chose the latter. It might at least give Trooper Nelson time to catch up with us, and maybe . . .

I went up slowly and came out in the dark at the top of the stairs.

———

I expected her to direct me over into that corner where she had left Amy's body wrapped in its rug, but she didn't. Instead, she forced me to climb the ladder that led upward to the widow's walk, the very highest part of my house.

At the top of the ladder was a trapdoor that was weather sealed, hinged, and opened out. It had no lock, for who would need one at that three-story height, with no access from outside, only from inside after two flights of stairs and a ladder?

"Open it and climb out," her voice demanded from halfway down the ladder behind me.

Then I knew I had a chance—slim perhaps, but still a chance.

Having lived in the house for so long that I could have found my way anywhere inside blindfolded, I did not have to feel for the flat boards placed on edge to form rungs for that particular ladder. Over the years I had climbed it often just to reach that high point and take in the magnificent view of the Kenai Mountains across the bay.

I also knew that the hinges on that trapdoor were strong and that one-handed there was no way to get easy leverage from the ladder under it, as the other hand must be used to hold a climber to the ladder.

So I lifted and threw back the trapdoor, scrambled out as quickly as I could, and, before she could reach the top of the ladder behind me, heaved the trapdoor back over the opening. Then I sat down on its unhinged edge, making it impossible to be lifted by anyone under it.

I heard her shriek of anger from below, but faintly, and soon, when she couldn't lift it, she was pounding on the underside of the obstruction she had not anticipated that I had placed in her way.

Then, for maybe a minute, there was silence before I heard the sound of a shot as a bullet punched its way through the top of the trapdoor.

How it missed me I have no idea, but it did. I didn't, however, make the mistake of retaining my seat there like an idiot to await the second one, which punched another hole near the first. Instead I moved to stand on the hinged side of the trapdoor, so I could push it down if she attempted to move it and climb out, also so that I had what little protection was available and could remain mostly unseen, especially in the dark.

She did not try again for the next few minutes, long enough to make me wonder what she would try next, for I did not believe she would give up so easily. So I waited, silent and unmoving, for I thought that if she listened carefully she might be able to hear where I was by my footsteps and aim another shot through the roof in that direction.

The night was still and motionless. Everything seemed to hold its breath, waiting.

Then, with a screech of tires, a police car swung into my drive from East End Road. From where I was I could see two policemen get hurriedly out and come trotting up the drive to vanish from my sight before they reached my door. Then I could hear them pounding on it and calling my name and Trooper Nelson's.

His car was not in the drive, but he must be around somewhere if they were shouting for him, I thought, wondering if he had heard my assailant's voice as well as my own on his cell phone. I hoped so, for then he would have known she was inside my house and would have taken precautions in entering and in finding her.

The answer came very soon.

Below me, on the ladder that led to the widow's walk, there was suddenly a knocking on the underside of the trapdoor.

"Maxie?" his voice called out. "Maxie, it's me, Alan Nelson. Are you up there? Are you okay?"

When I threw back the trapdoor his face rose into view as he climbed up and out to stand beside me.

"Thanks be," he said. "I was afraid she'd—"

"Came close. Tried there at the last, but didn't," I interrupted. "Where is she? Did you find her? I was afraid that when she couldn't reach me she'd find a way to lurk and shoot you. She was in the house, you know."

"I do now, but how were we to know that she was listening to everything we planned? I'm really sorry, Maxie."

"No need. But you've got her now, right?"

"Yes. They've got her—see? They're taking her back to the station for interrogation. The courts will get her on attempted murder in your case—probably murder in the two others."

He waved a hand toward the drive, and when I turned I could see her, a scowl on her face, hands cuffed behind her back, as they put her into the backseat of the squad car.

"Besides," he continued, "on the cell phone I heard just about everything she said—and everything that you said, of course. So I knew where she was taking you as you climbed the stairs. At least that much of our plan worked."

"Who *is* she?"

"We don't know yet, but we'll be finding out and I'll let you know. All her identification is falsely in Amy Fletcher's name, of course. But she must have come from New York and been good at tracking both John and his sister, considering that she wound up here in Alaska at the same time. It's her killing them that doesn't make sense. It'll come clear sometime soon, I hope, so like I said, I'll keep you posted. Let's go down. It's downright cold out here."

I knew his word was good—and that he was as good as his word and I would know soon everything I needed to know about the three people, good and bad, who had interrupted and threatened my life. How lucky for me that I got to know him and that he believed and cared about all of what had happened.

I went downstairs to find Stretch still shut in the office, so I immediately opened the door to find him lying directly next to it on the cold wood floor.

"Come on out, buddy," I told him. "All the excitement's over and you've not got to defend me anymore, okay? Come out and I'll give you a treat or two and some water."

He gave me a baleful glance as he came out of the office and headed for his food and water dishes. It was a look that pretty much said that he didn't understand how I could have done without his assistance in vanquishing the woman and her threats, but his tail wagged without his admitting it, and he licked my hand as I gave him a dog bone treat to chew on. That told me I was forgiven, but for a day or two he would watch closely to make sure I didn't get myself into more unnecessary trouble, without him to get me out of it.

Thank you, Daniel, for leaving me such a treasure as Stretch. He is certainly not really a bitser—which means mongrel to an Aussie—but calling him one periodically doesn't seem to hurt his feelings, so I guess he thinks it's high praise. He's never been a wanker—which is what they call a complainer. And thanks to Daniel's good sense in picking a dog, Stretch is dinkum—the genuine article.

———————

A couple of days later Trooper Nelson was back knocking at my door late one afternoon on a cold and cloudy day that threatened more snow in the offing.

"Got some very interesting news for you," he told me as he came in, sat down at my table in his usual chair, and nodded when I offered coffee. "Yes, thanks."

I joined him and settled in to listen, seeing the satisfaction on his face and hearing it in his voice.

"Her real name is Julie Webster and she's wanted in New York City for breaking and entering—you guess where."

I thought for a minute before saying, "Well, if I have to guess, I'd say probably John and Marty's apartment, after she died on nine-eleven and he took off across country, but before his sister followed him."

"Right on the money," he told me. "She and John worked in the same office and she was stuck on him. After his wife died in the destruction of the towers, I'd guess she thought she had another chance to fill the hole left in his life. Wasn't going to happen though and he let her know it. According to people who knew her, his turning her away for the second time infuriated her."

I nodded thoughtfully. "Given the circumstances, I've been thinking about it a lot and that kind of obsession may have come as a result of her rejection and the anger that grew out of her caring for him to begin with, don't you think? It only makes sense for her to follow him if she could continue to tell herself that she loved him. But she must have killed him because she was angry at his rejection. She must have followed his sister, the real Amy Fletcher, letting her do most of the tracking work. Was this Julie Webster really in love with him?"

Alan agreed. "Obsessed might be a good word. He had dated her, but broke it off when he met Marty. Evidently Webster didn't take it well at all. Decided to kill them both, but nine-eleven came first for Marty Fletcher."

I thought for a moment, then half smiled.

"'Hell hath no fury like a woman scorned,'" I reminded him. "And that's adapted from a play by William Congreve, which reads correctly as: 'Heaven has no rage like love to hatred turned, / Nor hell a fury like a woman scorned.'"

"Whew!" Then he nodded. "I guess that's as good a way as any to describe Julie Webster's anger *and* obsession," he said slowly. "God save us guys from furious, vengeful women, yes?"

———————

"Don't be a stranger," I told him at the door.

"Not a chance. Stay warm. It's going to snow again."

He gave me a salute, trotted off to his waiting car, and was gone down the road to the next law enforcement problem.

I went back inside to give Stretch his dinner.

Harriet and Lew were coming for supper.

Lew was bringing the wine and I had made another stew.

———————

They arrived almost together and we sat down to enjoy each other's company along with the dinner, but first I decided we needed a good toast.

Lifting my glass, I gave them a bit of Thomas Moore that's appropriate for those of our age:

What though youth gave love and roses,
Age still leaves us friends and wine.

"Hear! Hear!" said Lew, and we settled to small-town gossip at the end of the road . . . and good friends with whom to share it.